Golden Age

AND OTHER STORIES

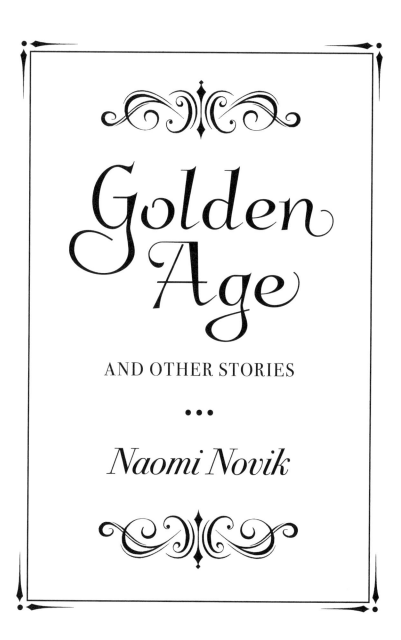

Golden Age

AND OTHER STORIES

...

Naomi Novik

SUBTERRANEAN PRESS 2017

Table of Contents

Volly's Cow

(art by Cary Shien)

EMERAIRE WAS REALLY QUITE FOND OF VOLLY—
no one could help being so, he felt, unless they were of
a particularly unsympathetic nature—but there was no
denying that nothing could claim a share of the little dragon's attention

whenever there was a cow in the offing, which he could reasonably have laid claim to, and sometimes unreasonably.

It was rather mortifying on this occasion, because Temeraire was not alone at all—he had brought Gaudion with him. This dragon was an acquaintance of Perscitia's originally from the eastern breeding grounds—an experimental cross between a Yellow Reaper and a Regal Copper, who had come out with both the wrong size and the wrong color, at least if you asked the British breeders. He was as inclined to be jealous of his consequence as a Regal, and yet wistful for company as a Reaper, an unfortunate conjunction of traits which had seen him given up to the breeding grounds without too much regret by the Corps, and there quite lonely, until Perscitia had discovered him in her efforts to find likely candidates to stand for the next election.

Gaudion was very much inclined to make a part of whatever party would have him, which Temeraire was not certain made much of a recommendation, but which Perscitia considered of the first importance—"We will never make much headway unless we vote as one," she always said. "We must make ourselves a reliable set of votes, so that *any* government that might take power shall want to make itself agreeable to us." Besides this, he was also reasonably clever, and sensible when anyone was not making him feel smaller than he thought himself, at least according to Perscitia. Temeraire had never yet seen it, himself, as evidently his mere presence was enough to put Gaudion's back up.

"And if nothing else, he can squeeze his head inside the building through the skylight, which you can't, and he *looks* like a Regal Copper, which will certainly have a good effect," Perscitia said.

"He does *not* look like a Regal Copper!" Temeraire said. "No one could possibly mistake him."

"No sensible person could, but I assure you there are any number of members of Parliament who *can*," Perscitia said firmly.

So it was desirable to have him elected, and in any case it was certainly more desirable than having no dragon elected for the seat at all. The lines of the borough had been drawn in a very awkward way indeed, carefully skirting the edge of the eastern breeding grounds, avoiding Dover entirely, and Perscitia had been at some pains to find any suitable candidate at all within their bounds. Only because Gaudion had slipped away from the breeding grounds and established himself in a small cave in the South Downs, after too many affronts to his pride, could he qualify, and now they must somehow find at least a few votes for him.

Which had brought them here: Captain James and Volly had only lately been stationed at Bodiam Castle, where they might serve as a longer-distance relay for Winchesters carrying messages from either London or Dover, and were just inside the borders. Volly certainly did not care anything about Parliament or the election, of course, but he had as much right to cast a vote as any other dragon, and Temeraire was sure he would be willing to oblige, if only he could be made to understand what he had to do.

And if only Temeraire could win his attention for long enough to explain it. But there was the cow, just the other side of the tall fence, chewing its cud meditatively. It had been hooded like a cavalry mount, a technique the herd masters had lately adopted which kept the cattle a good deal fatter and more complacent when they had to be raised near dragons. Temeraire had quite approved—it was a Chinese practice, which Laurence had passed along to the Corps through Jane Roland—until this particular moment, where the cow had quite of its own volition wandered right up to the edge of the pen, where sat Volly directly opposite, staring at it in unblinking and total focus.

"I am sure they will give it to you for dinner tonight," Temeraire tried again, "or at the latest tomorrow; you are sure to have a nice haunch of it very soon," but there was no use talking to him at all; Volly's head did not twitch away in the slightest. And the election was this very day—Temeraire had not thought it wise to try and instruct

Volly in advance, and rely upon his memory—and the voting should have ended long before feeding time.

Then Gaudion made things worse by saying, stiffly, "That *is* a handsome cow, and very large for such a small beast; I don't see why he should have it all to himself, when there are other dragons about, who have a just claim to a share," and Volly certainly heard *that*. He flattened his wings against his back and hissed at Gaudion, who drew his head back indignantly. He was nothing like a Regal Copper, but he *was* much bigger than Volly, of course, who was a courier-beast and closer in size to the very cow he was eyeing.

But of course, Volly was a working-dragon, and the cow was in his own feeding pen, and well within his rights. "*My* cow," he said, in tones of clear outrage.

"Certainly it is your cow!" Temeraire interjected hurriedly. "You have been flying a great deal lately, I hear, and you have earned it; *I*, for one, would never dream of encroaching." He fired a stern look at Gaudion, who scowled back at him sullenly, not recommending himself in any way whatsoever.

Then inspiration struck, and Temeraire leaned over towards Volly and whispered, "But I am sure *that* dragon might well try to be quarrelsome about it: shall I get him away again, before the feeders should get round to the butchering? He *is* a middle-weight, after all, and if he is here when they serve it out, he could certainly make some noise about it. Pray come and cast your vote for him in the election, quickly, and he will have to come away with me at once."

Planting Season

(art by Hugh Ebdy)

Author's Note: While Hugh's gorgeous picture depicts Laurence and a new-hatched Temeraire, for me it immediately evoked Boston Harbor, and so I've written about a very different character who hails from that region of the Temeraire universe: the American dragon John Wampanoag, introduced in Blood of Tyrants. *This story takes place a considerable time before that appearance.*

THE SMELLS OF BOSTON HARBOR WERE PRETTY extraordinary to a young dragon's nose, the tar especially, and John shook his head at the enormous sprawls of fish being heaved onto the docks in their nets, most of which already smelled old. But he marched onward anyway. The sailors who noticed him cleared out of his way all right, and a Narragansett man off one of the whalers called him a greeting and offered him a tasty thick slice of blubber, which you couldn't call anything but nice, even if it wasn't *perfectly* fresh.

"Do you know where I can find Mr. Devereux?" John asked him, and was pointed to the right warehouse: it had *James & Devereux* charmingly painted in gold across the façade in the crisp letters which John had been studying carefully with Father Duquet since his hatching. He couldn't have got through the front door, but there was a larger one in the back, where a wagon had been drawn up to be loaded, and a cleared spot round the corner where the horses couldn't see, with the marks of dragon claws on the ground. John settled to wait until the wagon and its big draft horses had cleared out, and then he went inside and spoke to the large man who had been directing the loading.

"I'm from Mashpee: will you please ask Mr. Devereux if he will speak to me? I have a letter for him from my chief." The men were looking all round him and even peering under his belly, like he was hiding a rider somewhere, so he put out his right foreleg and waved it to show the leather satchel bound securely around it.

"How do you do," Mr. Devereux said when he came out, very loudly and slowly, as though that would've done any good if John hadn't learned English in the shell.

"I am doing pretty well, thank you," John said, and introduced himself as John Wampanoag, since the colonists got fussed if you didn't use a last name, "and I would like a cargo, if you have one looking for transport."

Devereux soon began speaking in a more ordinary and sensible way, although it was clear he was perplexed because John did not have a rider with him. John didn't care to explain, though, so he only said, quite simply, that he did not have one.

"Anyway," John said, "I can carry more if I don't have a person weighing me down. I have flown as far as New York, and come back without any trouble," and handed over the letter from the sachem which expressed her confidence in his reliability, and more importantly an offer to guarantee two hundred dollars' worth of his cargo. He had proposed that himself: an amount judiciously chosen so its loss would not hurt Mashpee too much, but enough not to be thrown trivially away.

"Hm, I see," Devereux said, when he had read it.

John added, "I am no heavy-weight, of course, but perhaps you have a smaller cargo which needs to go right away, or can find one."

Devereux eyed him narrowly, and then said, "Well, let me see what I can do. Will you come back tomorrow morning?"

John spent the afternoon pleasantly, fishing for his supper in the waters off the harbor—no stale fish for him, thank you—and to make a nice omen of good fortune, in the late afternoon he spotted a whaler in the distance having a fight with a sperm whale a bit too big for them. He flew out and offered to help in exchange for twenty barrels of whale oil out of their hold. The captain bargained him down to ten in a shouted exchange, which was as much as John had really hoped for, so when the whale was secured, they parted with much satisfaction and a sense of a good bargain on all sides.

John took his ten barrels back to the docks and slept across from James & Devereux curled round them—no one troubled him at all—and in the morning, Mr. Devereux offered to buy them for twenty-eight dollars, which was not quite at the top of the market but a fair price.

"Perhaps you could make it a bit more, in shares of my cargo instead of cash: if you have found one for me, and would be willing to take me as an investor," John said, before Mr. Devereux had even brought out the bills.

"I suppose I can see my way clear to that," Devereux said, a bit bemusedly. He had four tons of tea to send. By some unlucky chance—for them—five different ships had made it into port from China that same week, and the price of tea in Boston had dropped low enough that Devereux had decided it worth buying some and shipping it on to New York. They agreed that John's share should be a twentieth of the cargo, along with a hundred dollars for carrier service, which was handsome. John had them bundle the sacks of tea under his belly and wrap it with a thick padding of oilskin to keep them dry.

The journey to New York was all right: it wasn't too cold anymore, and he found a nice sheltered clearing to pass the night halfway. A couple of Mohawks with riders who didn't look more than a week past manhood tried to give him some trouble over the Hudson the next morning, but John beat up into a tall damp cloud and hid for half an hour. They shot a few bullets idly in his direction, but they eventually lost interest and went spiraling away, so they hadn't seen he had cargo. It was all right to say they were one nation now, but there were plenty of folks who didn't care to remember it when they saw you crossing their hunting grounds of the last five centuries with something worth having.

Probably they had also seen that he hadn't any rider.

John dived out of the cloud and shook the drops from his wings. He didn't feel too cold in the chest or the belly, thanks to the oilskin, and looking himself over, it occurred to him that the covering made the cargo hard to see against his dark brown hide. Nobody would've guessed he was carrying four thousand dollars' worth of tea. He might get a cover made to match him even better, and harness straps, too. It would be worth the investment to get back and forth without trouble: having to stop and negotiate a toll, or worse, fight. Personally, he had never understood those dragons who liked a quarrel as much as a good dinner.

Singing Bird had spoken to him and his two hatch-mates about it seriously even while they'd still been in the shell. Fighting wasn't any use to the tribe these days. Yes, old Green Wing, who was getting on for two hundred, would tell you as long as you'd listen, "Before the yellow fever came, you could not fly ten miles along the coast without seeing a wetu from the sky, and there were a thousand men for every one of us," lamenting, "and they would dance and race and duel, and show their skills, and only the best were allowed to ride, and we would go on great raids, and bring back the tail-spikes of our enemies."

Well, that had all been over a long time before John had even broken shell. These days there were less than a hundred dragon riders left among the Wampanoag. Twenty-seven had died in the Revolution. And there were a lot of colonists with a lot of guns, all of them hungry for land.

The sachem Philip, Singing Bird's great-grandfather, he'd tried to chase them off, a little more than a hundred years back. He'd made alliance with the Narragansett and with the Mohegan, and together the dragon riders had run the colonists all the way back behind the long guns of Boston, and burned their farms. But the next spring, their King across the sea had sent a big red-speckled egg, and a year after that, Massachusetts Bay colony had a dragon bigger than any of the ships in their harbor. When Dominus went aloft, he took two dozen men with him, loaded down with guns and bombs. He could smash a whole village in fifteen minutes, and twenty dragon riders together couldn't say much about it. So Philip had to make peace, and they all sat down around a table and drew some new lines on some new maps, and then the colonists went right back to nibble nibble nibbling around the edges, anywhere there weren't enough Indian folks to catch them, which was everywhere.

When the Revolution came, there'd been a lot of arguing among the Wampanoag. Some folks wanted to help the British, who promised to keep the colonists out of Indian lands. But Singing Bird had stood up and said those promises weren't worth any more than the ones they'd got before now, and the colonists weren't going anywhere. Better to divide them from England with all its busy factories, and long guns, and dragons who could knock you around like a flock of chickadees. She'd already been sachem in Mashpee, since her father had died, but the Wampanoag had named her great sachem, after that, and gave her the name Singing Bird to mark it.

So the Wampanoag—and the Narragansett and the Mohegan, just about all the Iroquois, and eventually the Shawnee, too—had all gone in with the Revolution, instead. The colonists had made a lot of promises, too—Washington couldn't have made much headway without any dragons on his side—but it hadn't been so easy for them to go back on their word. Not a week after the smoke cleared at Yorktown, Dominus flew off to Halifax, along with Gloriana from New York and Solaris from Richmond. And young Tecumseh went flying all over the country: he'd come to Mashpee and spoken to Singing Bird, and by the time they were ready for the Constitutional Convention, he'd gone to Philadelphia with pretty much every dragon rider left at his back, and demanded seats at the table. Nobody had seen their way clear to sending him away.

So now Pokanoket was a state, and the other Indian nations were too, and most importantly, it had been written into the Constitution that nobody could own land in the borders of an Indian state, only the right to use it, and their descendants had to renew their land-use rights with the sachems whenever they inherited.

That had stopped the worst of the dirty tricks that the colonists had been using to get their lands, getting folks drunk and bribing them to sell land they didn't have a right to. But it wasn't going to save them forever. Singing Bird said they had just won some time: time to become the people who made the guns, and the ships, and wrote the laws. Only that would save them, not tooth and claw. That was what she needed them to do, she'd told all the hatchlings. It was hard for an old dragon to learn new ways, so it was up to them, the young ones, to learn English, and as much reading as they could, and put their brains and backs to new work.

John meant to do his best. His hatch-mate Pine Carrier had taken a young man from Cohannet as a companion, and they had gone into timber, where they could together work faster than any crew of twenty; when they had proven themselves, the village would go shares to hire their own crew and equip them, and give them logging rights in the Wampanoag woods. There was talk of a saw-mill of their own.

Wave Climber had also taken a companion: a half-Dutch, half-French, half-Mohegan—well, somewhere in there—first mate off a whaler, who had married a Wampanoag girl from Aquinnah; together they had hired on another whaling cruise, and the village hoped to arrange to buy a ship with them.

But John had no companion. After hatching, he'd asked Singing Bird for an English name, the plainer the better: it wasn't like he was going to be mistaken by anyone who mattered, and he figured if he didn't have a man to go between, at least he might as well give the colonists an easy handle to use for him.

He liked flying more than most other things, so he'd decided to try his hand at shipping. When he had built up enough of a nest egg, the Mashpee would stake him to open a trading house of his own. Or help him buy into one, maybe, it occurred to him. He'd tried Devereux to start because three separate Wampanoag traders had told him the firm drove a fair bargain and didn't pay Indians worse for the same goods as they did white men, which a lot of other trading houses did, and didn't mind loading and unloading dragons. Well, it was early days to judge, but John thought pretty well of the old fellow so far, and it stood to reason a house that could go between colonists and Indians and merchant ships stopping in Boston Harbor would be in a good place.

He flew on the rest of the way to New York City on a nice tailwind. There were other dragons at the docks and in the market there, including one big, stern-looking Mohawk who had clearly got some European blood in her with that tonnage and her round head, sitting at the end of Maiden Lane with a gold chain on, keeping the peace. John landed by her to pay his respects. "John Wampanoag, here from Boston with some tea for the market," he said in English, since he didn't know Kanienkeha.

The big dragon looked him over closely and then nodded. "The Mohawk buyers will take your goods."

"Thank you," John said politely, "but I'll try selling them myself, first."

She snorted. "White men don't know how to talk to dragons."

Privately, John figured that mostly white men didn't know how to talk to a dragon who could swallow them in one bite, and why they'd bred them up so big in the first place just to scare themselves with, he didn't know. Well, he knew, but it still seemed an awful waste.

Anyway, he looked round the edges of the market and found a few boys in a side lane playing some kind of a game with a ball and a stick, half of them with at least some Indian blood in them, and they were more than willing to give him a hand for the promise of a dollar apiece. They untied his oilskins and laid the sacks out neatly and started yelling at the top of their lungs, "Tea for sale, straight from China, shipped dragonback! A dollar a pound! Tea for sale!"

That was undercutting the prices John had overheard cried under the roofs, by a fair margin, and custom started coming his way. He didn't have a scale or bags, so he had the boys tell people to scoop it out roughly. He was losing a bit on each sale, but he figured it wouldn't really matter, and it didn't: in less than half an hour, a man came out from one of the biggest market stalls and quietly asked how much for the whole lot.

"I guess I could see my way clear to selling it for sixty cents a pound," John said, since they were selling it for a dollar-twenty under the roofs, and after a little back-and-forth they settled on fifty; which made his own pay $300 for four days' work. He did have to spend $20 of his money on his dinner, because he couldn't go hunting in Mohawk territory. But since he had to spend $20, he spent $25 instead, and bought himself a prime bullock in the market: those were going cheap pound-for-pound compared to the goats and sheep that would feed an ordinary-sized dragon nicely.

The Mohawk peacekeeper kindly told him about a nice sunning spot up on the heights near Fort Tryon where he could eat and sleep under the guns, with a peacekeeper dragon up there, too. John got the slaughterhouse to cut him up his cow, and he gave her one hindquarter and gave the other to the peacekeeper at the fort: that left him a still-glorious piece of rich fat beef that would feed him for three days even with all this flying, and well more than five dollars' worth of good will.

"You have good manners—for a Wampanoag," the fort peacekeeper said, and roared with laughter, startling a whole flight of pigeons off the nearest roof and making a dozen soldiers come running to see who had attacked. But then he invited John to sleep next to him right inside the fort itself, and he weighed at least eleven tons, so he could make all the bad jokes he liked. John ate his dinner and slept peacefully with his money under his belly.

In the morning, he flew back to Boston with the money: an even easier flight, with no weight on him; he slept just across the Connecticut border and reached Boston just before noon the next day. "You can leave my share right in that pouch," he said to Devereux. "Next time, if you like to trust me for it, I'll buy a cargo for the way back."

"Tell me when you'll come next, and I'll have a cargo waiting for you," Devereux said. He was pleased: he'd cleared three hundred dollars more on the load than he could've got in Boston.

They bowed, and agreed on Wednesday, the day after next, and John took his share, did a little shopping of his own, and flew back to Mashpee. It was getting on for sunset by the time he got home, and the cooking fires were making a glow in the houses and the wetu: the village was running about half and half these days. The warm good smell of corn porridge cooking was welcoming, even though he wasn't hungry yet after that huge meal, and when he landed in the square, a bunch of the children came running to greet him and climb on him and try to poke their fingers into his pouches. "Off you get," he said firmly, and told the oldest boy to take down the sack of candied flowers and marchpane fruits, and they all squealed with joy and started a fierce negotiation over how to dole it out amongst themselves.

Singing Bird came out of the big house, her warm brown eyes smiling at him. John ducked his head and said gruffly, "I brought some winter clothes, too, and tobacco, and tea."

"We're all glad you are back safely," she said, and put her hand on his side. Some of the other women took his bundles, and he let Singing Bird take the pouch with the money: her face brightened and a few of the worry lines smoothed out when she saw how much he had brought in. "I'll have time to go and bring in some game tomorrow," he told her, "and I don't need supper tonight: I ate like a fighting-dragon in New York."

"You need rest after a long flight," she chided gently.

"It wasn't so long as all that," he said. "Maybe I'll see what Devereux thinks about my going west, in a few trips. I could get twice the money for factory goods out in Ohio, I bet, if I take it in furs."

After dinner, she brought out the big Mashpee account book and the one she'd set aside for him, and sat beside him so he could watch her write the numbers all down. She closed the books when she was done, and put them aside, and sighed softly, looking west: the sun was ducking into the treetops. She smelled good, of earth: she'd been helping with the planting today, surely, like everyone old enough to put hands in the dirt and young enough to walk. "A messenger came from Tecumseh this morning," she said after a moment.

"Is it all settled?" John said, steady.

"Yes. The Shawnee have offered four eggs, and ten thousand dollars in gold. He will come when the planting is finished." She drew a deep breath. "We will live in Kentucky during the winters, and come north in the spring."

John didn't mean to moan about it. Wampanoag women weren't supposed to be dragon riders, anyway. Maybe they could have managed something if she hadn't also been a sachem, and if she hadn't been the great sachem, and if they didn't desperately need to bind the nations together, and if, and if. There wasn't much use in ifs. "Well, Kentucky's not so far," he said. "I guess they'll be wanting goods out there, too."

"I'm sure they will."

"Maybe you'd like to have a look at the fields, from above, and see if there's anything going wrong," John said.

"It would be nice, if you aren't too tired," she answered, a bit guiltily. It did all right for an excuse. She scrambled up onto his back, not at all like a steady, cool-headed sachem with a heap of responsibilities, and he leapt aloft with her. Even though he was tired, he spent all the hour she would allow herself up in the clouds, and she sang just for him in her deep sweet voice while he flew a long lazy spiral over the fields just peeking green in places, where the corn plants were breaking the ground.

Dawn of Battle

(art by Nick Miles)

Author's Note: Nick Miles' beautiful painting of an unfortunate ship of the line caught between two dragons and bursting into flames immediately evoked for me the famous destruction of L'Orient, *the French warship that exploded during the Battle of the Nile when her powder magazine caught. This story takes place in the hours before those cataclysmic events.*

JANE AWAKENED EARLY, ONLY A THIN LINE OF RED-GOLD at the end of the world below. She put out her hand automatically over her head for her boots, but remembered belatedly they were slung over the bottom of the hammock, where they would knock a midwingman's head instead of hers, during rolls: the captain's privilege of space. She pulled them on still lying on her back, shifted her carabiners to the climbing harness, and swung herself out.

A single glance below showed her that the ships of the flotilla were turning eastwards along the Egyptian coast, their lanterns a flock of fireflies turning away from Alexandria harbor. She went up the side, taking automatic note of the rhythm and pace of the wing-beats: Excidium was flying strongly and well, rolling through his strokes, no sign yet of tiring, although he had taken to the air seven hours ago, after only a pontoon-raft nap. The pursuit was going too quickly for their transport to keep pace, and the Egyptian countryside was by no means safe for them to put down.

Caudec was sitting at the neck, hunched in his leather greatcoat with his bristling mustaches dewed with morning mist. He saluted her indifferently and said nothing. "Any signals?" Jane asked. She oughtn't have had to ask, if there had been, but she knew what the fellow was about.

"Nothing to concern you," Caudec said, avuncularly.

"I prefer to concern myself," Jane said. "Ensign Bridely, light along the log-book there," she called. She had seen enough of this kind of business with her own mother, who had never managed to say boo to any of her own firsts. The mourning band was still black round Jane's sleeve, and the fierce grief still a lump in her belly, but there was no use pretending that Mother had not allowed herself to be imposed upon by a long procession of some of the most scabby officers in Christendom: including Caudec himself, who had been aloft with her these last three years.

Bridely, a boy of twelve, scrambled over with the log-book, although he darted a look at Caudec as he did, and well he might when Jane had opened it: *Sails to east, frigate* at the bottom of the page, not fifteen minutes agone, reported from that big Turkish beast who kept slipping out of formation and trying to climb overhead, instinctively.

"When next a man of war is sighted, Mr. Caudec, you will inform me directly," Jane said. "Who has gone to look in on them?"

Caudec, stiffening with indignation, said frigidly, "I beg your pardon?"

"No-one, then," Jane said, deliberately misunderstanding, and unhooked her speaking-trumpet. "Excidium, dear fellow, will you ask Glidius to take a quick dash eastward ahead of the formation and have a look round for us?"

"Yes," Excidium answered her, in his deep sonorous voice, and called to their Winchester courier, a clever little fellow as quick as a hummingbird, to go chasing the sunrise and the sight of sail.

Jane shut up the log-book and handed it back to Bridely. "I will stretch my legs a minute," and without giving Caudec a chance to launch into the speech he was plainly making ready, she set off at once on an easy clamber along the length of Excidium's spine: as familiar to her as the nursery of her own home, if she had ever had another. She had been kept on Excidium a long time as a child—longer than she had ought to, because Mother hadn't wanted to be parted from her. It had been her one and only rebellion; Jane thought of her again with mingled love and exasperation, irrepressible even in memory.

It was more than half the Admiralty's fault, of course. Their Lordships liked very much to put girls up green as grass whenever they had the chance, in hopes they would let some fellow put his hand on the reins. Jane's grandmother had been perfectly hale and hearty at forty when they had abruptly grounded her and put a timid seventeen-year-old on Excidium's back for no good reason.

Well, Jane was not a green girl, and certainly she was not timid, and she didn't mean to have it. She had put up with Caudec so far only because the Admiralty were already wary of her. She had formed a reputation enough herself, by seventeen, that no one had talked of retiring her mother in her favor, then or since. No, if the pleurisy had not carried Sarah Roland off, she would still be up here this very moment, with Caudec neglecting to so much as scout for French positions, even though he ought to have known, if he didn't, that Admiral Nelson was short on frigates, and would be glad of every minute of warning they could give him and his ships.

The sort of man who would take a post where his understood duty was to encourage his captain to be shy was not the sort of man to be trusted with the management of a Longwing, as Jane would have been glad to tell the Admiralty from long experience. She had watched them march through the post all her childhood, five rotters to one decent man, and the Admiralty had removed *him* after six months, because he'd been encouraging Mother to give more orders to the wing in flight.

Well, before Donoghue had gone, he'd told Jane quietly to make her mother send her to Kinloch Laggan to get her training begun properly, and to get her own childbearing out of the way early. Jane had been eleven years old at the time, but she'd already been capable of recognizing it as good advice. So Emily was three years old and thriving, back on their transport at the moment with her sensible nurse; and Jane had nine years under her belt studying with old Celeritas and occasionally serving with a decent captain when their Lordships would give her a berth. She knew her work, if she were allowed to do it, and Excidium was quite ready to support her.

They had spoken, after the funeral. The Admiralty could not spare him in the least with Bonaparte stamping all over Italy like a thundering colossus, but Jane had known that there were officers enough prepared to find consolation in grounding her, if Excidium did not like to keep fighting and chose to retire to the breeding grounds instead.

"And I don't blame you if you are tired of the whole business, after all these years aloft," Jane had told him forthrightly, ignoring the lecture she had been delivered by an entire panel of admirals reminding her to exert every wile and coaxing allure, as though she were some damned simpering maiden. "But we can ill afford to lose you. The French are talking quite seriously of coming across the Channel, one of these days," which no one had seen fit to tell him, idiotically, although they had told *her* to weep and wail if he so much as breathed a word of retirement.

So she had drawn him the map of the French coast in the dirt, which of course he recognized quite well, and pointed out all the places where troops had gathered. "And they have a second Flamme de Gloire hatched lately, of course," Jane said.

"Yes, I can see it would be nasty without me," Excidium remarked: he did not need it explained to him further. He rubbed the top claws of his wings together, thoughtfully, which he did when he was getting round to saying something; he was not a chatterbox, and would often go weeks in covert without saying a mortal word. Jane did not interrupt him, but waited, and at last he said, "I do not think dear Sarah was very happy in the Corps."

Jane still remembered the enormous surge of relief: so he did not *want* to go. "No," she had said. "I don't think you could find anyone less suited to the work than Mother, and it is a damned shame the way the Admiralty saddled her with a great collection of lumps. I will say, if you can see your way clear to sticking it out, that I don't mean to put up with it myself."

He had put his eye down to her close, inspecting, and she had put her hand on his snout, full of affection for the dear old thing: he had tolerated her swinging from his bone-spurs and making a portcullis of his teeth when she was not five years old. In the very bad days, when that scoundrel Davidson had been strutting and boasting from sunrise to sunset how Mother would do anything he liked, and spending his nights in her bed, Jane would creep out of the captain's quarters after dark and tuck herself in the little hollow between jaw and foreleg to sleep; Excidium had never turned her away, and the gurgle of the churning acids in their sacs was her idea of what an ocean should sound like.

"Yes, I will stay in harness; if you are certain," he had said, a shade of doubt still lingering in his voice.

"I am," Jane said. "I suppose," she added, "that those loobies at the Admiralty had a good shout at Mother, too, and told her she must swear to you up and down she wanted nothing but to go aloft, or else she should be a traitor to the crown. So she has spent all these years telling you she was delighted by it, and all the while you could tell otherwise." Excidium lowered the lids on the deep orange of his eyes, and said nothing, but Jane nodded. "Well, I will not lie to you, dear fellow, about this or anything else: I don't find it answers well, and I am not afraid of those sacks of wind. But in all honesty, I haven't the faintest notion what I should do with myself otherwise. I am as ill-suited for a domestic life as Mother was for anything else."

So she had her captain's bars and Excidium's wings at her back, and she did not mean to be cowed. However, she was not quite so angry as she had been, as a girl, so neither did she mean to pick a quarrel where it would not serve the Corps. Caudec was a lump, but he was not at least a scoundrel, or a disgrace to the name; she knew he had done serviceable work under Captain Lenton. He did not shine amid the firmament, and that had kept him from an egg of his own, so he had taken a post where he might be a captain in all but name. Jane could understand the choice; he had not done it out of liking to bully a shy woman. The men were kept in decent order, if all of them a bit dull, but no really good officer would be eager to serve on a mismanaged dragon, even a Longwing. Her wing-dragons had better crews, and Candeoris, the Regal Copper at their heels.

She would repair that, by and by. First it remained to see if Caudec could be salvaged, and she had an inkling that today would see that question answered. They had chased Bonaparte's fleet all round the Med now without yet catching a glimpse of them, but Jane felt in her bones the pursuit had drawn close. Alexandria harbor was packed to the brim with French transports, and the French had been here. This Nelson knew his business, too. If they could be caught, he would catch them.

Jane had seen from aloft his captains rowing day after day over to the flagship, and she had sent Candeoris's Captain Nutley down once or twice, since she could not go herself without setting up a great noise.

Nutley was not a lump, but he still did not like taking orders from a girl fifteen years his junior when Excidium and his own beast were not in the middle. However, Jane was prepared to use a few *wiles* for that: she had written him a letter asking if he would represent the formation, and write a note to all the captains afterwards with whatever he learned.

So she knew what Nelson meant to do, in nearly any circumstance, and so did his captains, and her own. She would have liked to hold like conferences herself, if she could have trusted her captains to come, but instead she had talked out her plans with Excidium, in the afternoons when Caudec took his sleeping shift. She would settle for managing the dragons, and let the men decide if they liked to be more than passengers aloft.

She walked back to the knot of the tailbone, with a nod to the riflemen, and sat there under the warmth of the climbing sun, letting the fierce wind of Excidium's vast wings stream past her until a slight increase came, a quickening of half a beat; she turned and saw Glidius winging back towards them at break-neck pace. She went back along Excidium's back double-quick, trusting her hands to find the harness-rings without looking. "All hands topside, Mr. Caudec," she said, again before he could speak: he had been stewing at the neck watching her all this while, waiting for his chance. "Bridely," she called, ignoring the gape Caudec gave her, "show Glidius a signal: *where?*"

Glidius had a young captain, a boy of sixteen as enthusiastic as you could like: he had his flags out and waving the first symbols of *French ships* already. Saved the trouble of telling them what anyone could guess, that he had found the fleet, he at once began spelling out the name. "Aboukir Bay," Jane said, recognizing the name when he was halfway through. "Bridely, ask him *how many, ships, dragons*, and then relay to the flagship and to the full wing: French fleet in Aboukir Bay, with numbers, and give credit to Bezaid for first sight."

Bridely did not hesitate; he had caught the excitement himself, and all the men in earshot; even Caudec had paused. She turned and gave him a hard look. "Mr. Caudec!" she said sharply, and he started, at last understood he must swallow his prepared lecture, and turning instead finally said to Lieutenant Gladstoke, "All hands topside, Mr. Gladstoke."

The men came swarming out of the belly-netting, half of them rubbing their faces. They were a slovenly lot: unshaven and half-dressed. Jane did not much care, except it gave her something to do with them. "Gentlemen!" she said, the trumpet to her mouth and her lungs behind it. "We have finally managed to corner the Frogs to give us a dance; before sundown this evening, if the wind does not change, and I trust every man aloft finds the news as welcome as do I. Breakfast at once, and coats and neckcloths all round: let us be presentable for the festivities. We will request pontoons at four bells of the afternoon, so Excidium can have a rest and a sup. You may cheer your dragon," she added, and after a startled moment they all shouted, "Excidium!" in tolerably full voice.

Excidium flicked his ears back, just a twitch, but enough she knew he had heard. "Pass the word for a steady pace, if you please," she called to him. "We have some young beasts along, who may need a reminder."

Candeoris was indeed creeping up on their tail already, as the signals were being passed along; Excidium did not speak, but flicked his own tail in a slight lash by way of hinting, and gave his wing-tips a quick flip on the down-stroke to mark the formation's leading edge to either side. It was enough reminder to the beasts, if not to their captains, and in a moment they had all settled nicely. The crew, too, had all made a dash for the belly-netting to make themselves presentable, and the duty officers were passing up biscuit and grog: the ground-crew had been left behind with the *Allegiance*, too.

Jane took a covered mugful herself, watered down by half on her standing orders, and went to munch her biscuit looking over the leading edge of Excidium's shoulder. The news had gone through the fleet below with as much energy: every vessel had pressed on a bit more sail, and she could see crews busy scrubbing the decks. "We are making a good time," she commented to Caudec, when he cautiously made his way out to her: she was balanced at the very edge where the chest sloped down and away. She did not remember any time before she had been used to sit so, but Caudec had come to the Corps at seven like most boys, and he had not gone aloft before twelve; besides he was not a young man anymore

"A word with you, at the tail," Caudec said, and reached out to put his hand on her arm.

She had half expected something of the sort. She had chosen the sitting place deliberately. The crew were most of them down below, and others at least plausibly out of earshot; he could not be humiliated, before the men, and kept on. She did not move, and only looked at him and said, "Take your hand off me this instant, Lieutenant, or I will have Excidium take you off and put you in the netting."

He halted, his face caught between anger and a sagging foolishness. He did not take his hand away at once, but he did not try to pull upon her, either, so she drew a deep breath, and thrust down the rising anger before it could climb too high into her gorge. Davidson was more than ten years dead, now, thanks to a French rifleman, and past anything she could do. She would not deal with Caudec as if he were the same man who had made her mother weep, telling her tenderly it was just as well she was in the Corps, and what a dreadful life it was for a worn-out woman otherwise without a man's protection; all the while taking her pay and making her say she was grateful to have him warm her bed.

Caudec was only used to think he might give the orders, and that he was the only one fit to give them; and he had been right, not very long ago.

"I am not my mother, Mr. Caudec," Jane said. "I am and I will be captain here. You must decide now if you will bear it, and be the officer and the bulwark Excidium and I require, without trying to lay claim to a false authority. If not, you go below, and I will leave you on board ship when we take flight for the battle."

He still hesitated. His mustache worked up and down with his mouth, but he kept in the spluttering; so she added, "You may consider this day a trial, if you like. I am sure if afterwards, you prefer to ask their Lordships for another post, they will have every consideration for your circumstances." The last dryly: the Admiralty surely owed him as much, having put him into them.

He swallowed, and then he took his hand away slowly from her arm. Jane nodded briskly as if he had just agreed with a whole heart. "Just as well: if I am knocked on the head in the fighting, I am sure Excidium shall be glad to have you aboard," she said, which would give him another scrap of hope to cling to. "Pray look in on our armaments, if you please; we must have fresh locks in all the incendiaries, and if we are short of powder or shot, we had better know it and send down word before the pontoons come out."

He did not say anything, but he nodded after a moment, and turned in his carabiners and went back towards the spine. Jane put him at her back again, and looked out ahead. She could see the ocean rushing away beneath them, and a tiny distant forest of masts and white sails standing in a line inside the blue cupped half-circle of the bay ahead. There were fourteen dragons sunning themselves on the shore, more than she had at her back. Jane smiled into the wind. She was not afraid.

Golden Age

(art by Sandara Tang)

TANG SHEN WAS VERY TIRED. THE SHIP WAS STILL sinking behind him, the hollow sound of its wooded sides beating against stone audible even through the roar of the storm. The dragging weight of the crate pulled upon his body at the other end of the rope looped around his arms, and he had been ill for three weeks now. The fever still burned in his forehead and ached in every joint even now being numbed by the water. But he had been champion swimmer in his village as a boy, before he had bent to his studies; he had been given his promotion and sent upon this perilous journey for that very reason.

In any case, he was the last of his companions left; they had all sickened with the same terrible fevers as the rest of the barbarian crew, and now the ship itself with all of those sailors was vanishing beneath the waves. He was the last hope of the egg's survival. He kept his arms and legs moving through the surf. Perhaps none would ever know what he did here; perhaps he would fail. But at least he would try.

Lightning flashes overhead illuminated the wall of rock looming to his right, but he caught a glimpse ahead of the pale white of an empty shore, sand reflecting the light. His strength renewed by hope, he gulped air and plunged beneath the ocean's tumult. He swam as many strokes as he could before surfacing, trying to clear the dark mass of the rock. One more gasp for air, and then he managed to kick round and into the small bay. The water calmed a few strokes further in, and calmed further quickly; when he put his head into the water, he could see darker shapes waving beneath him, a forest of seaweed growing from below.

The waves were helping him now, carrying him in. He stopped laboring and let them slosh his body forward, his arms moving in slow, dull circles. The ocean floor rose abruptly and caught his feet. He began almost crawling rather than swimming, grabbing at the floor and pushing himself along for a long way in the shallow water until he managed to stagger up onto his feet and gain the shore. The wind still blew fiercely, and the wide fronds of the trees overhead were lashing with a dull rushing noise, but he was on dry ground. He sat heavily at the base of a tree and began to pull in the crate hand over hand. It was nearly at the shore when his hands fell from the rope, and his head leaned back against the trunk of the tree.

When the morning came, the wind and tide had left the crate by Tang Shen's feet. His corpse was already beginning to bloat in the hot sun. Its rays also penetrated the waterlogged wood and slowly began to steam the moisture from the straw. It was pleasantly hot within the crate. The egg rested peacefully. The ocean continued to throw up bits of shattered wood from the wreck, scraps of sailcloth and rope, barrels and boxes marked *Amitié*.

THE CORPSE'S bones were mostly picked clean by rats and ants by the time the egg within the crate began to crack. The hatchling was not pleased to emerge into a thick cloud of straw, nor to find a thick wooden wall beyond it; instinct and desperation made his struggles vigorous, and he managed to tumble his crate over and burst open the weakened lid. The dragonet spilled out onto the sand and rolled over twice before sitting up on his haunches, shaking sand off indignantly.

To either side of him a small gentle curve of sand stretched away a little distance, quite empty. Ahead, the vast wide ocean ran dark blue to the horizon. Behind, a solid tangle of greenery and trees. He nosed curiously at the crate from which he had emerged, and the collapsing pile of bones at the other end of the rope, but neither responded. He looked round himself uncertainly. The silence seemed very peculiar. He had spent the last several months surrounded by the echoing voices of French sailors and Chinese attendants, the constant creak and groan of a sailing ship, the rise and fall of her rhythm on the waves.

"Bonjour?" he called at last, tentative. No one answered him.

But the eerie quality of his situation could not long compete for his attention. He was *hungry*, and there did not seem to be anything here to eat. He broke open several of the barrels, and found some soggy biscuit and some salt pork. He took a few bites of each, but their edibility seemed questionable. He flung out his wings and shook them, and after a couple of attempts managed to get into the air. He could not stay there for very long, but fortune smiled on him: on his third crash into the water, he knocked into a sea turtle. It was large and perplexed by the collision; the dragonet suffered no similar confusion. He immediately bit off the turtle's head, and then swam awkwardly to the shore dragging it along and spent the rest of a pleasant afternoon prying open its shell and devouring the soft meat. It was delicious.

As the sun went down he sat upon the shore looking out at the ocean in a more harmonious spirit. He sang one of the sailors' songs, without quite grasping what the words meant, because it was the only way he had found to make any of the friendly noise that had gone missing. And then he curled himself up and went to sleep.

A WEEK later, beginning to fly longer distances, he stumbled upon a cove with two other dragons in it dozing. They were roughly his size, and startled when he landed. They hissed at him at first, but he was carrying a large fish which he had just caught, and after a moment of thought, he carved it into three pieces, and shoved the other two portions over. He felt that no one could take that the wrong way, and his instinct was correct; after a moment, the other two dragons ate up their shares, and afterwards they spoke to him. He could not understand what they were saying, but then one of them said, very slowly and roundly, "Français?" and he brightened and nodded.

They took him a short flight to a much larger beach, where the rest of a flock of dragons were sunning themselves comfortably, and there introduced him to Galant. Very quickly the familiar sounds began to fall into place and take on meaning.

"But where did you come from?" Galant demanded, when shortly they could make themselves understood to one another. "You are nothing like the rest of us." He himself had been hatched in a French colony on another distant island, and had flown away because they wished him always to be carrying heavy loads, but he still looked like the local dragons, with longish scales in many bright colors: he said they were scattered all throughout the islands. "And what is your name?"

"Oh," the dragonet said, doubtfully. He vaguely recalled the voices speaking around him; had they called him something? "Céleste," he said after a moment. "At least, I think so. And I hatched on a beach over on the other side."

"Yes, but eggs do not sprout from the sand," Galant said decisively. He flew back with Céleste to the beach, and after a little inspection announced that he had come from a shipwreck, and undoubtedly the ship had been French.

"Not that you need take much notice of that," Galant said, with great condescension. "You are a free dragon now, and you can stick with me. I will translate for you with the others."

"That is very kind of you," Céleste said, although he felt privately that he would rather speak to everyone else himself, and not through an intermediary all the time.

He did manage to master the island dragons' language in another few weeks, which was just as well, because everyone was becoming quite disgruntled with him: he was still growing. Céleste tried to share as much of his catch as he could bear to, apologetically; he was conscious that he was taking rather more than any ten other dragons, and the others were making dark remarks about overfishing. But he was still hungry all the time.

He found a few signs of some other presence on the island as he flew across it, hunting: little decaying huts that someone had surely built, but when he peered inside, there was no one ever there. "There were people here, some time, I believe," Galant said. "But they were all taken away in ships." There were no large animals.

Increasing hunger at last drove Céleste to attempt a longer flight. "There are whales and sometimes even kraken, if you go out past all the reefs," Mikli told him: she was one of the island dragons. "They are so big you could not eat all of one," which Céleste was not quite sure he believed. Mikli was one of the quickest to talk about greedy persons, who liked to take so many fish that there were not enough for everyone, even though not long ago there had been *no difficulty*. But Galant agreed that one could indeed find enormous fish out in the deeper ocean. And it stood to reason, Céleste felt, that there must be something big enough to feed him somewhere.

He was still anxious about finding his way back, afterwards. There were no landmarks upon the ocean, and it seemed easy to get turned round. But the next morning he woke and found everyone else had got up quietly before him, gone on a frenzy of fishing and both gorged themselves and scared away all the fish from the local waters. Now they were all pretending to be asleep again. It was a perfectly clear message, and with feelings somewhat injured, Céleste decided he did not care if he did not find his way back; he could do just as well on another island.

He set off, therefore, flying straight out over the open ocean. A pang struck him when he looked back, and the island had become the faintest line on the horizon, but he took a deep breath and kept going until it vanished entirely. But his courage was rewarded: not half an hour later, he spotted something large and silvery ahead just beneath the surface of the water. He decided he would not risk waiting for a closer look; he folded his wings and dived for it at a steep angle, and his claws sank into its flesh.

The fish was indeed enormous: he had never seen anything like it. It was so heavy he had a real struggle to lift it, the whole shape peculiarly round and flat and bulging. It did not wriggle, but flapped its fins with alarm until he bit it several times, and it finally went limp. He ate and ate, hovering, until he discovered he did not *want* to eat more: a sensation he had not previously experienced. There was indeed some of it remaining. After a bit of consideration, he decided he *would* go back; he felt rather in charity with the world at present, and ready to be forgiving, since Mikli had *not* lied to him.

He did manage to find his way; some instinct guided his head despite the featureless spread of the ocean, and had the pleasure of landing on the beach with the remnant of his catch to the great surprise and loud admiration of the others: even what was left of his fish was bigger than anything anyone could catch in the bay, and certainly none of them could have managed it themselves. "Yes," he said, smugly, "you may eat it; I have already had my fill," even though they did not really deserve it; but everyone was very appreciative.

"It eats very well," Mikli said, "although it is not a kraken; *those* are even bigger."

"I do not suppose that anyone could really *want* a bigger fish," Céleste said coolly. "It would certainly go bad before it could be eaten up."

But he kept growing. He found another of the round-faced fish two weeks later, just as big, and ate it down to the fins every scrap. In between he was out every day catching other big fish in the open ocean, as many as he could, and he could not help himself; he ate them all without bringing back a single bite.

However, no one made any remarks anymore. Indeed, they had all become really quite respectful and polite.

Nevertheless, he was delighted on the day when at last he did encounter one of Mikli's whales. She nudged him awake that morning herself and said, "They are here! The whales are coming by, come and have a look."

They were not very far from the island, and there were several of them traveling in company, of various sizes: some were even larger than himself, and he was surprised to realize that he had not seen anything bigger than he was for some time now. He considered taking one of the smaller ones, but then he looked over at the island and judged the distance; he said to Mikli, who had accompanied him, "Go and bring anyone else who would like a share, to help." She had been circling overhead—the others did not seem to have the trick of hovering—and she dashed away at once, returning with a dozen of the others.

He picked out a large and sluggish member of the group at the end. "Go at the tail!" he called to the others, and they all latched onto the flukes in great excitement. Diving, he seized the base of the tail, closest to the body, and called, "Together now, pull!"

It took them nearly an hour, but they dragged the whale together back to the island and onto the shore. It was so enormous they all feasted themselves to their swollen-bellied limits, and then Céleste permitted the rest of the dragons to come and have a share, even if they had not helped. "But next time," he said sternly, "anyone who does not help shall not have a share, unless they are sick, or if they have done their part another day. And," he added, "we will think of something to do with the leftovers."

"We might try drying it," Galant suggested. "I have seen men dry fish, and eat it again later."

They sliced it up with their talons, and tried to hang it on trees; they did not have much luck, however, and four days later, it rained and all the meat began to stink so dreadfully no one wanted to try eating it anymore. But that was all right: they threw it in the waters a distance off the island, and so many fish came to eat it that they all took their fill, even Céleste. And when next they wanted a whale, everyone did come to help, anyway.

The days rolled away with placid sameness. Céleste's appetite at last began to slacken; he still wanted a big meal every three days or so, but he was not so hungry all the time. "You have got your growth, I expect," Galant said knowledgably, and everyone expressed their relief in loud congratulations. Céleste was so big now he covered a considerable stretch of the beach at night. Galant was the largest otherwise, and Céleste could have spanned his entire back with the talons of one forefoot. A round dozen of the others slept on his back at night, and more curled up round his sides, all of them pleasantly warmer as a result.

But as his hunger faded, he began to feel increasingly restless. "No, I am not hungry; only, what is the use of just lying here all day?" he said, when the others asked why he was getting up, and whether he was going hunting again.

"I will go with you," Mikli said. All of them had for once had enough to eat without having to work very hard for it, and with food grown easier to come by, several of the others were also willing to join him in exploring. They flew idly round the nearby islands, but found nothing much more exciting than a herd of iguanas disinclined to make room on their beach.

"You had better be glad not to have found any trouble," Galant said. "Stay away from the bigger islands! You may be sure if you came on some men, they would straightaway try to put you to work. It would be ropes and chains and lectures, all day." Céleste could not really muster up any fear: anyone who had lived in those little huts could not alarm him. But that was hardly a recommendation to seek out such rude people, either. He could not have named what he wanted, he only knew he was dissatisfied. He flew further and further each day out over the open ocean.

Three days later, he went whale-hunting again with his friends. They were all of them still well-fed and full of energy, dancing around the clouds, and it was such a lovely day for flying that even after they spotted the pod, they did not immediately pounce: they were far enough away from shore it would be a long flight to drag their prey home, and no one was in a rush, least of all Céleste. Instead they flew along, playing games of tag and fly-the-loop, and suddenly Galant said, "Ah! We should get our hunting done and get out of the way: look."

A very peculiar thing had appeared on the horizon, something rather like a dragon lying on its side in the water with one wing sticking up, only it had many wings, all white, and they were not flapping but just belled out with the wind, and it was not a dragon. It did not look like anything Céleste had ever seen. "What is it?"

"It is a ship," Galant said. "And when they see us, they will certainly fire a gun to chase us off. Don't get too close!"

Céleste was more interested than alarmed, and he turned aside from the whales and instead followed the ship. He could see it was made of wood, and when he peered closer he could see many little creatures swarming over it, which he supposed were men. He thought of going lower and trying to say hello: according to Galant, they could speak, and if they had *made* this ship, they were surely very clever, and perhaps interesting. "Do you think they will know French?" he asked.

"I do not know, and I do not want to know," Galant said decisively. "If we are not taking a whale, I am for going home."

"Well, I will try, at least," Céleste said, and he dipped from the clouds and dropped to hover before the ship, calling, "Bonjour!" as loudly as he could.

A great noise arose from the ship at once, but none of it sounded like an answer. Céleste winced. All the men were scurrying and running and shouting; some of them had brought out long things that shone silver in the sunlight and were waving them in the air. One of the men, with a magnificent and enormous growth upon the top of his head that made it larger than any of the others, shouted something over the rest of them. It did not sound quite like French at all, unfortunately, but Céleste saw that a great many of the other men were moving quickly in response, and pulling forward a large peculiar tube of black, housed in wood, to the front of the ship.

"I told you, I told you!" Galant cried from above, flying anxious circles. "It is a gun! Come away!"

Céleste was cautious enough to dart to one side when the thing made its loud roaring noise, and *something* came flying past him, so quickly he could not make it out or see where it went, except there was a terrific splash as it landed in the water, flinging spray so high it spattered him where he hovered.

The men had also brought out several long sticklike things and pointed them at him. These made loud popping noises not quite as unpleasant as the big gun, but something spattered hot and horribly unpleasant against Céleste's leg from them, and he cried out and jerked back in surprised dismay and pain. All the men aboard began shouting again, in a jeering sort of way, and there was—there was blood, spilling from his leg, and in outrage and indignation Céleste drew a deep furious breath and roared.

He had never roared before; he had never felt impelled to do so. But it came quite naturally. The roar burst from his chest and the whole ship heaved back from him as if carried by it: the gun rolled backwards into the men trying to put another lump of metal inside it, and went flying down the length of the ship; the nearest of the tall spindly trunks shattered, and its huge white wings came sinking down upon the heads of the men with their popping sticks. Screams and yells rose up.

Other men began to fire more of the popping sticks at him from up in the other trunks. Céleste backed away, rather taken aback by the result, but Mikli had dived down roaring herself to his aid. She squalled as one of the men managed to hit her, too, directly in the shoulder, and she fell out of the sky onto the deck.

The men began to leap upon her with their silver things, and Céleste realized after one terrified cry from her that they were like claws; the men were cutting into her body. He roared furiously again and flung himself upon the ship: he seized upon the largest trunk and wrenched the whole thing bodily around until it cracked and came up from the deck, and then he flung it with all the men aboard into the ocean. Lunging, he snatched more of them by handfuls and threw them off, knocking a dozen of them off Mikli with one swipe.

The other dragons poured down to help, grabbing men by the shoulders and carrying them off, and then the rest of the men were all leaping away overboard: they had a couple of smaller wooden hollow things, which they heaved into the water, and the men crammed themselves aboard these and began to use long sticks to push themselves away from the ship.

Céleste paused, hard of breath; the ship was creaking and wobbling beneath him. All the men had vanished, except for a last few diving off the back of the ship; he paid them no attention. "Are you all right?" he asked Mikli.

"No!" she said. She was making small miserable cries of pain, and when he tried to get her upon his back, she shrilled and refused to be moved. Finally Céleste gave up, and seized up all the ropes he could find lying about and dragged the ship through the water towards the island.

The others all took a rope and helped him, but it was still very hard going. But at last they reached the bay again, and Mikli was persuaded to crawl off the deck and onto the beach. She lay down with an air of martyrdom, and they all anxiously inspected her wounds: only to find nothing but a few superficial scratches already closed, and one small puncture in her shoulder, which was barely bleeding anymore. "Well, it was very painful!" she said defensively, after they all upbraided her for giving them so much work and worry.

"And now we have nothing to eat, either," Galant said. "Well, we may as well see what is inside the ship: they may have some kind of foodstuffs in there."

Céleste pushed the ship over, and all together they pounded it up and down against the rocks until the hold cracked open, like a turtle shell. But no food fell out. Instead, with a rumbling clang, out spilled a heap of small bars of some dazzling, brilliant stuff, blazing through the water in the sunlight, and as they all drew in a single united gasp of admiration, Galant said, "Gold!"

CAPTAIN LAURENCE let the last page drop to his small desk, frowning. He had read for the twentieth time through all fourteen separate accounts of the pirates with the enormous black dragon, from twelve separate incidents, and he remained dissatisfied with his intelligence. Though several reported being hailed in French, not a one offered the slightest description of ship or sail to guide him to his enemy. As far as anyone might have told, the dragon was appearing full-blown from the depths to punish greedy mortals for their sins, as the especially fanciful account of the Leander would have had it. The reports had almost all come from sailors on merchantmen, of course, whom Laurence did not entirely trust to provide a reliable account of a battle, but the captain of the ill-fated *San Esteban* had been a former Spanish naval officer, and a British privateer had also been among the victims.

Laurence looked down at the pages strewn across the wood and then with decision swept them into a drawer and stood up. He went out onto the deck of the *Reliant*: his first lieutenant Riley was on duty, and saluted as he came out. "A fair wind, sir," he said. "I think we will make Bermuda by morning."

"Good," Laurence said. "You will oblige me by arranging a standing guard with pepper guns, henceforth, and we will bring up ten of the twenty-fours to the quarterdeck." Riley looked dismayed, as well he might: more than half their guns. But there was no sense keeping themselves ready to meet a ship, when no one had yet managed to counter the dragon.

Laurence began to suspect the attacks no work of France after all, whatever the Admiralty thought. He discounted the tales of the dragon's immense size by a considerable margin: he had fought under aerial support three times in his career, and he was well aware that even a tidy light-weight combat beast easily gave the impression of hideous scale when it was flying directly overhead, roaring. The coloration, by contrast, seemed to him entirely likely to be fixed accurately in the mind, and the French did not have a solid black dragon breed. In any case, certainly it passed the bounds of credulity that a dragon transport could escape notice.

More likely some crew of outright pirates had by mischance managed to put their hands upon the egg of a fighting-dragon, or some larger breed native to the Americas. Their ship might well be a mere afterthought, a brig or something like, easily-overlooked in the confusion of battle and dismay. They would be making their home in some deserted cove or bay, near enough the site of the various attacks to put them in flying range.

He laid out his thoughts to his officers the following night over dinner, as they rode at anchor in Nassau harbor. The attacks made a relatively small knot of marks upon his map, which he had rolled out over the cloth once the dishes were cleared. "I am not inclined to assume we will have an easy time of it, gentlemen," he said. "I think we can trust the *Quickly* to have given them a respectable fight, and her twelve guns ought to have been enough to scare off any ordinary feral beast. We will double the watch in the tops, and furl our sails on any cloudy day."

Three weeks crossing the Caribbean Sea back and forth was productive of nothing but the corruption of some of his crew, overcome by the easy availability of women and liquor from the bum-boats that swarmed them anytime they came near enough a harbor. In exasperation after having been forced to put in to Nassau again in order to deposit ashore not one but three separate ladies-of-pleasure who had been secreted aboard, one by an over-ambitious midshipman of thirteen years of age, Laurence ordered his ship to remain closer to the uninhabited islands further from any source of such irresistible delights.

The following morning he was rewarded by the shout of, "Wing three points to starboard!" while still at his breakfast. Laurence made himself finish the swallow of his tea before he rose and put on his sword and went out onto the deck, his steps quickening involuntarily. The watch officer was standing at the starboard rail with his glass and pointed Laurence to the sighting.

The dragon in the distance was however only one of the ordinary ferals, brightly colored and courier-size at best, sporting idly over the waves. Laurence lowered his glass and rested his fists against the rail, considering. The beast was already darting away into the distance, vanishing to the east.

"Just a stray, sir?" the watch officer ventured.

"Very likely, Mr. Rawls. But it seems far from land for so small a creature to merely be entertaining itself. Set the course east by south, if you please, and we will beat to quarters," Laurence said.

He kept the ship on alert as they followed the small dragon's last course. Laurence studied the charts in his cabin; the Great Caicos and the Turks Islands were in the general direction, and had no settlements: a hospitable home for a pirate band.

They did not have to sight land to find the pirates, however. By mid-morning another shout went up from the look-out, and Laurence went back on deck to find every man staring silently into the distance at the crowd of dragons approaching, small as a flock of birds except for the enormous shadow in their midst, its wings wider than the full length of the *Reliant*'s deck.

Laurence stared also, in astonishment more than horror: it was certainly a heavy-weight, as big a dragon as he had ever seen. How had it ever fallen into the hands of pirates? But that question immediately faded in importance. "Launch the ship's boats with three pepper-men aboard to either side, and let us elevate all the guns. Reef sails."

When the dragons were close enough to hear it, Laurence ordered the starboard bow-chaser fired as a warning shot. It did not halt the beasts, and as they drew closer, Laurence swept the ocean behind them with his glass again and still saw no sign of any ship, no matter how humble: the day was clear and he had a clear view of the ocean's wide and empty expanse in every direction. Still more baffling, when the dragons drew closer, none of them had a stitch of harness anywhere to be seen, even the gigantic black one.

"Mr. Riley, let the pepper-men stand ready. The gun crews shall aim for that beast in the center whenever it should come on their side," Laurence said. "Hold fire until I give the word, and afterwards each crew is to fire independently until the order to halt is given."

"Very good, sir," Riley said, with commendable steadiness.

Laurence went to the front of the ship and turned round to face the men. "You were at the Battle of Vigo Bay, Collins, I believe," he said, addressing the chief of the first gun-crew.

"Aye, sir."

Laurence nodded. "The beasts do make an astonishing noise: not quite a broadside, but enough indeed to shake any man's spirits, if he had not heard them before."

"I'll take their bark over their breath, sir, begging your pardon," Collins said readily enough, to suppressed and nervous mirth.

"Indeed," Laurence said. "Fortunately, by all report none of our visitors have fire or vitriol to alarm us. I am sure mere roaring will not unman the crew of *this* ship."

"No, sir!" and "Hear, hear," were his satisfactory answer, and Laurence nodded and turned back to face the oncoming wave, his hands clasped loosely behind his back. A handful of the smaller dragons had now outdistanced their enormous companion and come darting towards them, circling them at a range which should have put them beyond the reach of carronades such as the merchantmen might have carried: a piece of strategy which gave Laurence fresh cause to be surprised and also wary. Their own long guns would have reached further, but Laurence was not tempted to give the order: he did not mean to give away the extent of their range only to strike a few featherweights. Behind him he heard the officers saying, "Steady there, steady, men; no firing until the captain gives the word."

The huge dragon came on for the head of the ship, and then abruptly checked his way, also just past carronade range, and hovering there announced in clear and carrying French, "Hello; you may begin firing now, or just get into your boats and go away, as you like."

Laurence stared doubtfully. It had never occurred to him to hold a conversation with a dragon; he had the vague understanding that it required some particular training, unique to the Aerial Corps. But the beast was perfectly intelligible, and there was certainly no officer or crewman aboard the dragon to speak to otherwise.

After a moment's hesitation, he borrowed the master's speaking-trumpet, and put it to his lips. "I am Captain Laurence of His Majesty's Ship *Reliant*," he called back, clearly, in his best French. "If you are the pirates who have been molesting the shipping in this region—" Here he hesitated, puzzled briefly how to proceed: it was nonsensical to threaten to hang a dragon. "—then I am charged to bring you to face the King's justice. If you surrender at once, you and your company shall face a fair trial for your crimes."

"Oh!" the dragon said, indignantly. "Our crimes, as though you did not always begin firing your guns at us straightaway." Then the dragon paused and said in suddenly uncertain tones, "Are not you going to fire upon us?"

Laurence began to wonder whether perhaps some clever and unscrupulous French officer had hit upon a scheme to set feral dragons upon enemy shipping without involving his own ship in any risk. "If you do not mean to surrender, I will certainly take whatever measures are required to halt your thievery. Who has instructed you to attack passing ships?"

"No one instructed us," the dragon answered. "I only tried to say hello, because I was curious, and they fired on us at once."

"And that welcome, I gather, induced you to return again and again, to other ships?" Laurence said dryly.

"Well, if you should *choose* to challenge someone, by firing guns at them," the dragon said, with what Laurence could only describe as a guilty air, "it is only your own fault, if you lose your treasure. I am sure it is not *our* fault if we are better at fighting."

A few of the other dragons, flying in their circles, jabbered at the big one loudly; he answered them in their own tongue, with as much fluency as the French he spoke. Laurence took the chance to consider the situation. He had never seen a dragon so close before, nor imagined that they could converse so intelligently, nor that they should offer quarter, or care to make excuses for their rapacity. Riley had come to his side; Laurence said to him quietly, "Have you ever heard it said that dragons are moral beings?" Riley shook his head helplessly. Laurence himself would not have previously imagined it, but the dragon seemed eager to defend the justice of its behavior.

"And why are *you* not firing your guns?" the large dragon pressed. "None of the *other* ships behaved so."

Laurence regarded the beast. He could not say that he was at all sanguine about the prospects of defeating a heavy-weight on this scale with a single frigate of forty-eight guns. At best, they might bring the beast down and themselves be brought by the lee in its vengeful death throes. But entirely aside from such considerations, he found something distasteful in firing to destroy so magnificent a creature, without the necessity of self-defense to impel it. As peculiar as he found the notion, if the dragon had enough idea of justice to wish to excuse itself, perhaps it had enough to be persuaded it had done wrong, and must stop.

"This is a fighting ship of the Royal Navy," Laurence said after a moment. "You have been making your assaults on helpless smaller merchantmen, whose crews are not trained to do battle. Naturally those men were frightened by your approach: you can scarcely deny that you present a warlike appearance, and you alone likely outweigh any vessel you have come upon, before this. You ought to be ashamed to have frightened them, and still more to have taken their panic as an excuse to rob them."

Some of the men had enough French to follow him, and most of the officers; a titter went round the ship when he had made this speech. "I've heard of men as would talk the birds from the trees, but not before dragons from the air," he overheard O'Dea muttering, on one of the nearer gun-crews, subsiding when reprimanded for insolence by Lieutenant Davies. Laurence himself hardly knew what to expect in answer to such an argument.

But the large dragon drew his head back as if he had been struck, putting his large frilled ruff—Laurence could not remember ever seeing a similar decoration on any breed—almost flat against his neck, rather like a horse putting back its ears. He did not immediately answer. He seemed dismayed more than angry, however, and Laurence entertained the notion that perhaps his persuasion had made some good effect.

But the small dragons yammered at him again; the big dragon answered them with a preoccupied air, his head bowed on his neck. Evidently growing impatient, one of the smaller beasts turned its head and hissed to the others, and five of them swarmed round and came diving in towards the ship. "Mikli!" the black dragon cried out, but the smaller beasts paid him no attention.

"Pepper away!" Laurence called, and heard the order go down the ship. The pepper-men in the tops immediately began to heave their large sacks high into the air above the sails, letting the corners billow open as they reached the top of their arcs, filling the air with such a cloud that Laurence presently had the peculiar fragrance of the spice in his nostrils. In the boats, the pepper-men took aim with their crossbows, launching smaller sacks into the air to either side. They went to their work with such alacrity that a greenish cloud filled the air before the first beasts stooping reached the masts, and no sooner had their heads come into the pepper than they began wincing away, shrilling unhappily and fouling one another in a frantic attempt to get away.

Even after they had retreated, however, the effects continued to make themselves felt: the dragon pepper was meant to act even upon much larger beasts than these, and Laurence had purchased freshly milled stock with his own funds, rather than rely upon the more dubious supplies provided by the Royal Navy. He was rewarded amply now by seeing the rest of the small dragons highly dismayed by the cries of their fellows, the leader of whom even plunged towards the ocean to thrust her head beneath the water, trying to wash away the contamination.

"What have you done to them!" the black dragon cried.

Laurence turned back and said dryly, "If they choose to fly themselves into a pepper-cloud, it is surely no fault of *ours*; do you disagree?"

As though abashed, the dragon did not argue, and abruptly he stooped—with astonishing swiftness, seeming even quicker than the little dragons though so far beyond them in size—and snatched up the still-crying small beast from the water where she was still trying to duck her head, and turning tail flew away at so rapid a clip that he left Laurence and the rest of the dragons equally startled. The rest of the dragons—there were not more than a dozen—looked down at the ship, as Laurence looked up, and then as if noticing they were out of their weight class flung themselves hastily after the black one, who was shrinking rapidly into the distance, heedless of their calling after him.

TWO WEEKS hunting through the nearby islands had not produced any sign of the dragon pirates, though Laurence had put in at every likely beach and cove which came in their way. At last Riley returned from another unsuccessful visit to one of the Caicos to report something of interest, and took Laurence ashore in a strikingly shallow bay: even the boat grounded nearly forty yards from shore, and they had to wade the rest of the distance to the disgust of several stingrays.

Laurence knelt at the side of the disintegrating corpse: very little left of the poor fellow but a skull collapsed into the hollow of his own ribs, and a few bones of the arms and legs scattered beside the hips. What might once have been a stout rope lay frayed into pieces round him and the weatherbeaten remnants of a crate lying upon its side, with the lid missing and several gouges of nails to show where it had been forced off. Inside a lining of waterlogged and ragged silk partly still covered a mass of thin and rotting straw, and upon the silk lay several large fragments of a thick, white eggshell.

"Yes, I fancy we have found the origin of our beast," Laurence said. "Have you anything else?"

"Only this, sir," Riley said, and showed him a weathered piece of a barrel they had dug up from the far side of the shore, marked *Amitié*.

"But where should they have been bringing the egg?" Laurence asked, half of himself; it was absurd. No dragon so extraordinary would be shipped to the colonies, and where else had any French ship in this part of the world any business to be going? "Let us have this crate over, I think," he added, and found his answer on its underside, where wind and sun had not faded away the elaborate paint and the markings which he recognized as Chinese script.

"They must have paid a fortune for it," Laurence said, blankly, and then looked up as a vast dark shadow fell upon the beach. Half the men cried out and fled crashing away into the underbrush, in a pardonable panic, and Riley drew his sword—uselessly, of course, as the black dragon settled directly into the shallow waters of the bay, clouding them with immense gouts of sand, and lowered his head towards them.

Laurence was not too proud to admit his back required stiffening, but it got the dose it required; he did not mean to meet death cowering, if it were at hand. He said quietly, "Mr. Riley, you will be so good as to take the rest of the men into the brush, and get under cover."

"Sir," Riley said, hesitating, but Laurence waved him back, and stepped towards the enormous head himself.

"It *is* you again," the dragon said in oddly wary tones, drawing back. "What are you doing here?"

"We have been pursuing you," Laurence said, and gestured to the crate and the shell. "Were you hatched here all alone?"

The dragon looked over at the crate. "Yes, but I did not mind it so very much, once I caught a turtle, and then I met my friends. I do not understand, why have you come after us? I left you alone and did not attack you at all."

"You have given no sign you mean to stop pillaging other ships. I cannot hold you so guilty for your piracy as I would, if you had been raised by civilized people and taught to know better. But you cannot be permitted to carry on in this fashion."

"I am sure I do not know why not," the dragon objected, in pragmatic tones. "Who is to stop me?"

"If your conscience will not do it, I will try myself," Laurence said, despite the patent absurdity of such a threat, "and if I am slain in the attempt and my ship sunk after me, a larger will be sent, with British fighting-dragons aboard it: there are some who outweigh even you. Sooner or late you will end as has every pirate chief whose rapacity grew so large as to make them infamous."

"Oh!" the dragon said, but then hesitated and a little diffidently asked, "Have you seen other dragons like me, then?"

"I have never seen your like," Laurence said. "I suppose," he gestured to the crate, "that you are Chinese; they are by repute very fine dragon breeders. But I have seen Parnassians, and Longwings, and a Flamme de Gloire—which are like to you in size, at least, and trained for battle."

"Well, I am sure I could learn anything they know, and I do not think I have done so poorly, considering there was no one to teach me anything at all, but Galant and the others," the dragon said. "But what do you mean by *Chinese?*"

Laurence hesitated, and then taking up a stick made a rough attempt at sketching for the dragon a map of the world, carved into the sandy shore, although he was unable to satisfy himself with his outline of China: he had only the slightest notion of that country's extent, beyond its coast. "How clever that is," the dragon said, meaning the map; he almost immediately understood the intent, which was not wonderful when one considered he must have been used to see the land from far above. "But I do not recognize the shapes of any of those islands. Where is this one, pray tell?"

He seemed rather staggered to understand that they were at present upon an atoll so small as to represent not a single pebble upon the sketch, and in a position halfway round the world from his origin; but he did not express disbelief at the scale, only rather plaintively asked, "But how did I come to be so far away?"

Laurence could not satisfy him on this point, and it evidently disquieted the dragon; he sat with head bowed in silence and then as abruptly as he had come launched himself with a terrific spring into the air and flew away, setting the bay sloshing so that a wave of near six feet managed to heave itself out of the shallows and swamped Laurence head to feet, drenching him entirely.

THEY SAILED round the island cautiously, the next day, and by afternoon the lookout made the band of dragons at last at their home, a truly grand sweep of sand the color of pale cream, many miles long, and the immense black dragon curled round himself halfway down. Behind him, heaped untidily upon the shore, an almost equally immense heap of dazzling gold and silver mingled here or there with some chest or barrel, a fairy-tale hoard with a heap of cannon stacked round it in what seemed a decorative spirit, and the wreck of what looked a dozen ships or more littered the beach at either end—their holds had evidently been broken open by banging them on rocks, rather like an otter with a clam.

The small dragons set up a tremendous alarum on catching sight of the ship in turn, and the black dragon raised his head from the sand. He leapt aloft and flew towards them, halting a good distance away, evidently grown wary of the pepper guns; a crowd of the littler ones followed him, although they made their limit at an even better distance.

"I am *not* letting you take our treasure," the dragon said defiantly, hovering.

Laurence, equally appalled and staggered by the scale of the plunder, found this a point not worth the argument; he could not have carried it all away if he had five ships the size of the *Reliant*. "The treasure is the least of it!" he said. "Can you look upon the wreck you have made of so many seaworthy vessels, and take any pride in what you have stolen from them? I do not suppose all the treasure you have amassed could pay for the damage you have done."

The dragon looked puzzled over at his own handiwork. "Do you mean, those ships? But they are only made of wood; they are not treasure."

"I do not suppose that the smallest ship wrecked on your shore was floated for less than three thousand of those gold coins you have piled there so untidily," Laurence said flatly.

"What?" the dragon cried, and reeled back so aghast it seemed Laurence might as well have ordered the guns fired upon him; he seemed truly overcome, and flew at once to the nearest heap of wrecked ships and from there in an arrowing line to the second graveyard at the other end of the beach, and back again twice; at each halt he went circling round and round over them as though completely out of his head, and at last came darting back to the *Reliant* to demand, "Can they be fixed? Surely they are not *wholly* ruined. Oh! If only those men had said anything! I would never have done it, never, never."

Laurence had to be glad to have made so profound an impression, although he would have preferred a different foundation for the dragon's regrets. Even the smaller beasts, when the black dragon had explained matters to them, grew astonishingly distraught; after they too had proceeded to visit the wrecks, they flung themselves upon the bobbing hulls very much as might a man upon the ruined stones of his house, brought low by fire, or sat upon the sand of the beach gazing at them with dull blank eyes and wings drooping limp, a picture of despair.

"We will never hurt another ship," the black dragon desolately promised, and while Laurence would scarcely have trusted the word of any other pirate, he found himself inclined to believe it despite the prompting of his better judgement. He consulted privately with himself that evening as the *Reliant* rode at anchor out from the bay, waiting for the morning's tide; he feared that he rather *wished* to believe, than did so on sensible grounds. But at length he made himself satisfied: the black dragon had given no proofs of *dishonesty*, in any of his actions, and indeed any rational consideration should have made lying quite unnecessary to so dreadful a beast, who might far more easily disregard any complaint than thus seek to evade it.

"I do not, however," he told his lieutenants the next morning, "mean to set up my judgement over that of Their Lordships. We will return first to Bermuda, and from there I shall send them my report; until we have word that they are satisfied, we shall remain near and continue to patrol the seas, and escort any British ships through the dragons' flying-range."

His officers were disappointed, he knew; they had naturally hoped to find some French privateer loaded down with treasure, a lawful prize, and at worst to return home and be set loose upon enemy shipping again. The *Reliant* was a splendid sailor, fast and graceful and well-armed, and fought well could reasonably hope to take most enemies in her class, and outdistance any beyond it. Fortunately, as a counterbalance to these regrets, no sensible officer could have looked upon the black dragon and wished very much to engage it with no aerial support. But Laurence steeled himself to be instructed to do just that, when dispatches came: the Admiralty had not sent him to preach, but to punish.

The *Reliant* passed three months sailing the Caribbean without serious incident: his log held in it a dozen meetings with merchant-men, none of them molested by the dragons, who were their only other encounter, and frequent enough to make amends for the absence of any other. He was at first wary, when a wing appeared off the ship's bow in a clear morning, but it was only the black dragon, alone, and he halted well off and called, "Pray may I come in closer? I do not mean to frighten you, at all."

"You may," Laurence said, after a brief hesitation; the guns were loaded, and the danger to the beast greater than their own, if he were trusting foolishly.

But the dragon indeed offered no attack. He only winged in quite near—his enormous scale all the more dismaying when he came so close to the *Reliant*, and it was evident that he was longer, nose to tail, than the entire ship. Then hovering there he put out his head and anxiously peered at the mainmast, tilting his head one way and another, much to the frozen alarm of the boy in the crow's nest, until Laurence asked, "What are you doing?"

"I am trying to see how it ought to be arranged," the dragon answered. "We mean to fix the ships, of course, only it is quite difficult when one does not know how it is to be done. Pray will you tell me, what are all these ropes for?"

Laurence did not in the least object to the dragons occupying themselves in such a project, however unlikely to succeed, nor to furthering that end, but he was puzzled to explain a ship's rigging in French. He was forced to make his apologies after a halting attempt, and then the dragon astonished him by saying, "You may as well teach me your language, then; I suppose it cannot be much harder than the one Mikli and the others speak."

Laurence supposed otherwise, but that struck him as a still better method of occupying the beast's time; he therefore arranged over the objections of his officers to go ashore in a boat once a day, when the *Reliant* was near enough some islet, and give the dragon lessons. He privately liked the arrangement for entailing a risk only to himself, commensurate he felt with the degree to which he was willfully indulging his own judgement. But before a month had passed, he was forced to confess, astonished by the progress and the wit of his student, that he liked it for its own sake, and indeed had begun to forget that there was any risk at all in the company of a dragon nearly eighteen tons. Céleste was too innocent of malice and fear alike to be a true object of dread when one knew him, Laurence felt; he suffered a daily increasing dismay over the prospect that the Admiralty might order him to make an attempt to bring the dragon down.

Even his crew had begun to grow fond of what they now called "the captain's dragon" with a hilarity that Laurence deliberately did not notice; he preferred them to be amused at his expense rather than frightened. If Céleste should come before he was on deck, some of the men would even speak with him, and the dragon was very ready to answer as his English improved; he was especially fond of poetry and recitations, when he could persuade any of the men to favor him, and the crew were at the same time engaged in putting on a performance of Macbeth, which aroused his interest so greatly that he began to come whenever he hoped a rehearsal might be in train, and listen raptly.

An anxious merchantman having demanded their escort some distance into the Atlantic, Laurence had not seen Céleste for three days; they were sailing west once more when a sloop hailing them in the distance proved to be just out of Nassau, and her captain informed him they had left his long-awaited dispatches with the governor. "I thank you," Laurence said heavily, and found it a great effort to maintain the conversation at his table, having invited the captain to join him and his officers for dinner.

"Have you had any luck chasing down those Frenchmen with their dragons?" Captain Archbold asked, innocently heaping coals upon Laurence's conscience. "I tell you, I do not suppose I am more of a coward than any man, and I have never met a storm yet to frighten me, but I saw a sea-serpent in the Pacific once, gliding past my ship, and if I never see another it will be too soon. It makes a man's blood run cold to think of going down the gullet of one of those beasts. I shall be very glad to know they are no more."

"We have found them," Laurence said, "and there are no Frenchmen: it was a pack of dragons, alone; a French shipwreck left the egg of a large fighting-dragon upon the shore, and his presence emboldened them."

"Good God!" Archbold cried. "A heavy-weight? —How did you manage it, with no cover yourselves? I should not have supposed a ship could come away so unscathed as you are."

"We have not found it necessary yet to fight the beast," Laurence said, and one of his younger mids piped up, with a giggle—he had drunk two glasses of wine—"The captain has tamed him instead!"

He was at once frowned into silence by the company and shushed by his neighbors, but Archbold looked quite astonished, as well he might. Laurence saw him off and stood on the quarterdeck alone for some time in the night air, silent and distressed; he felt abruptly how wrong he had been, to make a pet of the dragon he had been ordered to slay— and yet even this was false; it was impossible to describe Céleste so, as though he were a dog or a favorite horse. The dragon was his *friend*. Nor could Laurence merely reproach himself with self-indulgence, and feel that his pain was his own fault. Céleste had repented of his crimes, and ceased to commit them, as soon as he had known better. There was no justice in putting him to death, and less honor than that in betraying him and taking him by surprise, which certainly the only way in which an attack could succeed.

Laurence realized to his increasing horror that indeed, he could not stomach the act at all. He envisioned Céleste winging over the ocean to join them at midmorning, as was his wont, fearless and unwary— imagined his own voice giving the order to fire—the dragon falling broken to the waves—

It was impossible. He could not do it. He would have to return to England having failed in his duty, and submit to court-martial; some other man would be sent to destroy the dragon instead. And he would succeed, surely, for Céleste no longer thought to fear a British ship—unless Laurence warned him. His stomach clenched on the thought, still more a dereliction. But he could not persuade himself it was wrong. He would have to tell Céleste to hide forever, from all men of war, and never approach them again; and then he would have to submit himself to the justice of the Navy.

He could hardly claim to be indifferent to the prospect of ruin and disgrace, but a grateful calm descended, as soon as he had reached this conclusion, which assured him he had found the most honorable course amidst the shoals. He straightened his shoulders and went into his cabin, and at last was able to sleep; until just before morning a tremendous lurch heaved him out of his cot and onto the floor of his cabin with the lamp rolling by. He automatically put out a hand and caught it, blowing out the flame, and in the dim grey light heard the cries of his men mingled with a more hideous groaning of wood.

He waited only long enough to put on his boots; he thrust open his door only to find it partly barred by some heavy weight, as though a mass of cable had been flung across the threshold. He seized his sword and hacked at it, meeting only the resistance of flesh, and abruptly the shadowy mass moved away. He was able to push the door open far enough to emerge onto the deck, to find more long lumpy shadows strewn across his deck, and the lookout above crying out, "Kraken, sir! Kraken!"

The sun was coming up behind an overcast sky, lightening at great speed, and the dreadful beast's head was rising to meet it on the other side of the ship, vast nacreous eyes taller than the ship's anchor bulging from either side of a gaping, toothed maw. Laurence hacked grimly away at the massive tentacles as they swarmed among them, men tripping. The kraken certainly had mistaken them for a whale; the creature was so large nothing else could have made the bulk of its diet. It pressed its enormous mouth against the side of the ship repeatedly, evidently trying to bite. Finding nothing to satisfy, it pulled away and an enormous mass of smaller tentacles burst lashing from beneath the row of teeth and began groping over the deck and into the gun ports, curling around men and dragging them down into the monstrous gullet.

"To the guns!" Laurence roared again to any man who might hear him, carving away as he did a slab of another tentacle, trying to make his way towards the nearest gun. The kraken's shorter limbs were a writhing thicket in his way, and he had now to regret the guns he had moved to the upper deck; the guns on the lower deck might have more easily been fired against the beast. But he could not reach the ladderway, either; one enormous tentacle almost the height of his waist lay athwart the cover, the translucent greenish-black flesh pulsating with the blood vessels within.

A shadow moved across the deck, drawing Laurence's eyes upwards, as another monstrous limb rose from the depths and was flung over the ship. It landed with a terrible shuddering thump that nearly threw him off his feet, bearing away two of the spars. The *Reliant* groaned pitiably beneath the weight as the kraken heaved itself still further from the depths and up the side of the vessel, bearing her over. Under such a pressure the ballast would soon begin to shift, and the vessel be dragged beneath the waves as much by her own weight as by the monster.

Laurence snatched a second blade, slicked with blood and the monster's fluid, from the deck, and threw himself at the nest of tentacles, hacking away furiously. If no one could reach one of the guns, in moments more they would have tipped too far, and the guns would be firing against their own weight. Three crewmen fell in beside him, and they carved a path towards one of the guns half buried beneath investigating tentacles. He crushed smaller ones beneath his feet as they chopped away the larger, and reached the gun: he dropped his swords, and lashed himself to the carriage with one of the ropes wound half a dozen times around his body and passed it to the next man.

One of the younger ship's boys, a nimble creature named Flynn, came squirming up through a gun-port with a sack of powder held in his hand; Laurence seized it and thrust it into the cannon's mouth without benefit of sponging, and heaved the wadding and the ball behind it at once, and rammed them all down together recklessly. Together he and the men put their shoulders to the gun and ran her out with a groaning effort. Laurence ignored grimly the looming eye that rolled like a dreadful moon towards them, and the tentacles that wrapped round his arms and legs: the kraken became their assistant almost, dragging at the gun as well as them, and at last she was out and aimed towards the monstrous body of the beast.

Laurence began to try and strike the match. The rope round his body drew tight, as on the other side of the gun the gunner's mate Groghan was seized and lifted aloft, his hands grasping vainly for the carriage—he screamed as the tentacles tugged on him, digging the rope into the flesh of his thigh and waist. Boyle seized the rope and pulled back, braced upon the gun, and behind him, O'Dea had the quill into the touch hole, and the match began to smoulder; Laurence waved the other men back and stood himself with the linstock until they had cut themselves loose. The rope cut, Groghan was lifted away into the air crying out with the end dangling; Laurence set the match to the touch-hole. A moment went by, another—had the powder got wet?—and with a roar the gun fired, jerking Laurence entirely off his feet.

The kraken made no cry itself; the *Reliant* cried out for it, all the great tentacles convulsing and tightening upon her. Loosed, Groghan fell and landed upon the ship's rail and scrambled frantically over it and over the deck, slipping and scuttling hands-and-feet away from the wild thrashing of the kraken's smaller limbs. Laurence hauled himself up, ears ringing, through the cloud of smoke. The ball had struck the kraken's body and gone in, a puckered mark on its side scorched black at the edges, but it looked dreadfully small against the mass of the creature, and if the wound were mortal, it would not be immediately so.

The kraken heaved three more tentacles onto the ship, exerting itself to finish off its recalcitrant prey, and pulled itself still further up: the great maw gaped over the rail, and the deck began to tilt so steeply Laurence was hanging from the gun ropes more than standing. Half a dozen of the tentacles were coming for him, and the swords had slid away; he had a smaller knife in his boot, which he stabbed at them as best he could, and beat them off.

"Laurence!" a loud ringing voice called, over the screams and groaning of the wood, and Laurence looked in some confusion only to realize it was Céleste calling as the dragon plunged from the sky and struck at the head of the kraken. Even he was smaller than the leviathan, but he clawed it dreadfully, and with a darting strike of his head seized one of the tentacles in his jaws and bit it through with a violent snapping shake of his head.

"The one abaft the mainmast!" Laurence shouted, through cupped hands, sacrificing himself to the grasping tentacles to make the sound carry. "Strike there!"

Céleste twisted his head round and saw the tentacle, one of the largest, and the one which Laurence judged holding the kraken most securely to the ship; he struck at it with both forelegs, and tore it with his jaws. The kraken flailed at him, but he persisted, and worried his way through the entire limb. The kraken slid partway down as the loose end of the tentacle slithered off the far side of the ship, and the *Reliant* straightened a little in the waves, but the kraken's weight dragged down two of the topsails, gripped by its longer limbs, and caught Céleste's left wing in sailcloth and rope. He tipped over himself, and came nearly down upon the *Reliant* and the kraken, his flapping attempts to get loose only tangling him further, and the whole entwined mass of ship and dragon and monster rocked violently, threatening to doom all of them together.

And then Céleste spread wide the ruff round his neck and roared down directly at the kraken: a noise so violent the whole sea round the creature hollowed out to a deep concavity that bared its lower body and the seething mass of tentacles yet beneath the surface. The force of the roar traveled with visible rippling through the kraken's flesh, bulging it out, until with a shocking eruption the entire head of the beast burst entirely.

The remnants of the kraken's body sank at once beneath the wave. The tentacles collapsed limply where they lay, or fell overboard. The *Reliant* tipped so quickly back upright that Céleste was flung down into the water, and still trapped began thrashing, threatened with drowning, and began to scrabble at the ship in his alarm. "Hold still!" Laurence bellowed, himself snatching up a fallen sword as he struggled free. "Céleste, you must hold still, or you will have us all down!"

"I will try, only this is very unpleasant!" Céleste said, but despite his panic managed to hold fast to the *Reliant*'s side without thrashing. She tipped heavily under his grip, but he was buoyant enough that when Laurence had directed him to stretch his body out into the water—surrounded already by a truly frenzied crowd of sharks, who made him yelp unhappily when they mistook his talons for parts of the kraken—they were able to right themselves. Round Laurence a dozen eager hands joined in the work of cutting the ropes loose from the ship, and he climbed out onto Céleste's neck and there managed to cut away the worst of the sailcloth trap.

The surface beneath his feet lurched as soon as the fabric had slid free, and Laurence had to grab at the few remaining ropes as Céleste launched himself off the ship into the air with a furious beating of his wings. The world spun violently round as Laurence clung to his meager handhold, his body stretched upon the scaled back and his boots skidding over the surface as they lifted away from the poor *Reliant*, mauled and ragged amidst the wreckage of the kraken with so many fish feeding on its mass that the waters round her were gone silver with their bodies. Wind tore at his hair as the dragon wheeled round, and, breath stolen, Laurence saw beneath him the ocean spread out impossibly vast curved over the surface of the earth, and unsighted islands green in the distance.

"Oh, is it you?" Céleste said, peering round at him with one cocked eye. "Whatever are you doing there?"

"My best not to fall," Laurence shouted back; but the dragon was leveling out, and he managed to lash himself on a little better, with some of the cords he had not cut. It was nothing like a secure perch, but an irrepressible exaltation rose in him as though it wished to lift his breastbone out of his chest.

He had to shout to Riley, climbed up to the tops, to send a boat for him to the nearest atoll: there was no very reliable way for Céleste to set him down on the deck, nor could he simply dive off and swim to the ship with the infestation of sharks all round. Céleste set him down on a beach not far away, however, and when they had bathed thoroughly—they had both been thoroughly besmirched by the innards of the kraken—they settled together upon the sand to wait for the boat.

Laurence put his hand on Céleste's foreleg; the dragonscale was warm and living to the touch, resilient but not hard. Gratitude warmed him through, at unexpected grace: the *Reliant* would certainly have been pulled down, if not for the dragon's help, and Laurence would unhesitatingly have sacrificed life and reputation to save his ship and crew. He could not help but feel that he had been offered a test, unknowing, and having chosen to spare the dragon at that cost, had found himself rewarded for it. He knew it irrational, but he could not repress the sensation.

"I cannot say that I am fond of kraken, even if they *are* bigger than whales," Céleste remarked. "They do not taste nearly as nice, and are much more quarrelsome. But that was very exciting," this on a faintly wistful note. "Of course I do not want to ruin any more ships, and you needn't think I would ever break my promise, but it is quite boring only sitting round an island all day." He sighed and put his head down.

Laurence paused and looked over at the dragon. "Céleste," he said slowly, "would you ever think of joining the Corps? The Aerial

Corps, I mean," he added, as the dragon looked over at him. "As a fighting-dragon."

"Oh!" Céleste said, with dawning excitement. "Like that story you told me, of Vigo Bay!" He had been very enthusiastic about any stories Laurence could tell him of dragons in battle. "I might go to the Corps?"

"I have never heard that dragons are recruited to the service, being rather hatched into it, but I cannot suppose that they would refuse you, were you willing. It will be a puzzle to get you to Europe," Laurence said. "But I suppose it might be managed with a pontoon-raft, if a little awkwardly."

"I should not like to leave Galant and Mikli and all my friends," Céleste said, after a moment's consideration, "but I dare say some of them might care to join the Corps too. And you would be there, of course."

Laurence opened his mouth to say he was a naval officer, and not an aviator; but he found he did not wish to make his excuses. "I will certainly see you there," he said slowly. "I am afraid I do not know how captaincy is managed, in the Corps; there may be a question of seniority. I am in a different service."

"Well, I do not care how they have managed it," Céleste said firmly. "If they do not want to let me have you, I suppose we may always go on somewhere else, mayn't we? But I must think what to do with my treasure. Of course I will not take all of it away from the others; I do not mean to be greedy, and everyone else did help, but I do not suppose anyone can argue that *half* of it is mine, at least."

Laurence laughed suddenly; he supposed that with a fortune on the scale of Croesus even a dragon might be welcome wherever he liked to go. "Only you will find it difficult to transport," he said, amused.

"Oh, no," Céleste said, serenely. "We have got five of the ships afloat again. I have not thought of anything to do with them, before, but I am sure they will be very useful now."

Succession

(art by Stephanie Mendoza)

THERE WAS NO SHORTAGE OF WARNING. QIAN BEGAN to feel vaguely unsettled even before the decorations had entirely been cleared from the celebration of the egg's formation. She had chosen to begin early in the spring, with the approval of the court physicians and astrologers, and by the time the flowers had finished dropping from the plum trees in the palace gardens, she was certain. She watched the petals floating past her pavilion on the drifting current of the water, ephemeral, and said nothing to anyone. There was nothing to say, she told herself. Perhaps she was mistaken. So much could yet go wrong.

But the days marched onward and no mischance occurred. And she could not regret it. But she knew that others would. So she said nothing. Her companion was gone, her Emperor, her beloved Hongli with his cool wisdom and stern majesty; he was gone. His son was kind and all that was respectful, and she honored him; but she could not open her heart to him, and he had his own companion. She kept the secret like a pearl held in the mouth.

The first storm of rejoicing had passed. Now a mood of suppressed anxiety surrounded her. Her attendants sang peaceful, calming songs each morning and proffered the very best the palace kitchens could produce, carefully supervised by the physicians: cooling sherbets, heaps of fruit and grain, and light repasts of fish and fowl with all the bones removed.

The Emperor had not wished to ask it of her, but there was no other choice. Her grandfather Lung Tien Fai had been too old to try even during her own Emperor's illustrious reign. Her uncle Ming had never sired an egg, and after the disgrace of Prince Yunreng, Zhi had not even been willing to try. He had bought his prince some freedom by agreeing to stand as the Yongzheng Emperor's companion at his coronation, but it had only ever been a polite fiction, and ever since Yunreng's death, he had refused flatly to emerge from seclusion, or to have anything more to do with the world. It had required some twelve years of matings on her brother Chu's part, with twenty-three separate Imperial concubines, only to produce poor, ill-fated Lien. No one could ask him to try again after such a disaster.

And Chu's egg had caused her own mother's untimely death, hardening in the sac. Xian had clawed herself open to save it being crushed during the laying, after the physicians refused to act. The egg had survived, but infection and fever had taken her not two weeks later. No one had forgotten the dreadful event. No one spoke of Xian in her hearing these days at all, full of worry and superstition.

But Qian thought of her a great deal. As the weeks crept onward, she spent most of her days in the Pavilion of Ten Thousand Springs, which had been her mother's favorite retreat, although she knew her attendants were dismayed. She watched the reflections of the willow trees shivering in the water, and remembered her mother gazing just so, after Chu's egg had first formed.

Qian had long respected her mother's courage, but with a faint sensation of doubt. She had of course shared all the natural feeling for a fragile, helpless egg which any person of propriety and honor ought to have, but Xian's choice had not seemed the course of true wisdom. Surely the better choice would have been to release the egg at once, when it had shown the first signs of untimely hardening, even if its development was not so far forward as it ought to have been. The shell might have been reinforced with clay, and an attentive watch would have been kept upon it day and night. And Xian herself would have been preserved for both the sake of the nation and for the chance of another attempt. The most eminent scholars and physicians had so concluded, in the study that her emperor had ordered during the aftermath of mourning. Qian had seen no reason to question their findings.

But now she understood, and understood also her mother's silence.

When the weather turned towards summer, the Emperor sent the court physician to address any concerns she might have over the development of the egg, with his compliments. She was in the garden again when the attendants came to inform her that the physician was at the gates with his retinue. She should have sent for him before, she knew. Entirely aside from the anxiety over her health, there were many political considerations. She might put those aside now, with her Emperor in his tomb, but others would not. Even in her general retreat, she had heard the whispers moving through the court, with increasing force: no egg had formed, it had all been a sham; the line of Celestials was failing; there would be no companion for Prince Mianning. Many whispered it with malicious glee.

In resignation, she told her servants she would receive him. She returned to her pavilion and allowed the physician to examine her.

He put his hands upon her hide and palpated with exquisite caution, putting his ear horn delicately against her side and closing his eyes to better hear. Her attendants were all waiting anxiously, and his own servants and apprentices also, and relief passed over them like a visible wave when he announced beamingly, "The egg is exceedingly well-formed, and of a charming size," meaning that it was small, but not dangerously so.

But he was not the imperial physician for nothing: he continued along her side, feeling for the extremity of the sac, and his smiles abruptly faded. Qian lowered her head and did not look round. He continued to feel over her side carefully, and in a moment he said slowly, "Celestial one, may this humble physician inquire if it is possible that a second egg has formed?" He knew, of course, that she would know.

"Yes," Qian said. "Perhaps you would be so kind as to inform the Emperor."

He bowed and departed immediately, of course, with all his retinue. Qian said, "How hot it seems to me suddenly. I would be grateful of some cool refreshment," and her attendants all hurried away at once to prepare and to gossip, where she could not hear them, and left her to her privacy, at least, even if they had taken the secret from her at last.

The days afterwards seemed to roll away with enormous speed. The diet prepared for her shifted from day to day with the unseen arguments of the physicians; once she even came to her pavilion a little early and found the servants hastily clearing away one breakfast uneaten, and laying out another of entirely different dishes. For a week, they pressed enormous meals of stewed marrowbones and crushed bone upon her; then fear of early hardening reasserted itself, and all meat disappeared for another week.

Qian nodded when the scholars came to offer her their advice, ate what seemed appetizing, and ignored the rest. She had long since learned the virtue of refusing to argue. If she felt particularly hungry for something, she whispered a quiet word to dear Princess Hexiao, who had come to bear her company; she had been one of Hongli's favorite daughters. The dish would appear without ceremony, beside the delicate spray of the willow trees. The eggs continued to develop together, in harmony. She could feel the heartbeats like small urgent messenger drums accompanying the thunder of her own, fading gradually away as the shells thickened. Increasingly, she did not fear.

The laying became nearly an anticlimax. She woke in the early hours. She rose and went outside into the deep, cool water of her bathing pool, let it cradle her, and the eggs slipped easily and quickly forth, floating to the surface. Stars yet lingered in reflections around them. They had remained a little smaller, but she nosed them over with satisfaction, rolling them over in the water: they were both perfect. Then she raised her voice and called to the attendants, who came out rubbing their eyes and stumbling in the dark, and only belatedly fell to their knees and began singing a welcome to the eggs, while the cushioned carts were hastily rolled out so she might lay the eggs one after another onto their waiting beds.

She spent the next week in a mindless joy, coiled around the precious eggs. Many came to pay their respects, but she could not have said who came and who did not. Of course she noted the occasion when Prince Mianning came. He had expressed his gratitude to her before, when she had first chosen to make the attempt. Now he came and prostrated himself, formally, and asked her permission to see the eggs. He gazed upon them both and said, "They are equally splendid, Celestial One. Indeed, they appear quite identical."

"Yes," Qian said, still too happy to think, and unable to restrain herself from boasting, "I do not think anyone could find anything to criticize in either."

He prostrated himself once more before departing, and said nothing else, but by that afternoon, disquiet returned. She looked upon her two eggs, her two magnificent eggs. No one had found anything to criticize. They had been examined thoroughly, with strong lights shined briefly through the shell: two male dragonets, both well developed, mirror images of one another; and their hides were quite plainly dark. No one but herself could even distinguish between the two. That one had been laid some three minutes before the other, and there was a faintly different shade to the speckling developing upon the second egg's larger curve where it had occasionally rested against the bone of her hip. No one else seemed able to perceive the difference, however.

She did not choose to have an opinion on the fiercest questions presently dividing the court. Prince Yongxing had on several occasions probed her thoughts, and she had admitted him to her company and allowed the attempt, but she kept those thoughts deliberately unformed. She had met some few of the Europeans who had come to pay their respects to the Emperor, of course; she had many handsome gifts from them displayed in her private collection, in particular one charming toy of a miniature clock which on every hour opened its face to allow a dragon to emerge and sing a peculiar and incomprehensible song, to nearly inexhaustible hilarity. But that did not shape her feelings towards them. She understood quite well the concerns which had made her Emperor deny them the closer intercourse with China which they desired, and those concerns had not been diminished by the passage of the years.

But Hongli had once said to her, reviewing another lavish tribute, "How many gifts they have sent this year! It seems to me that the ships that come must be larger than when I was young." He had been an old man then, grey in the garden beside her; he had already formally retired from the throne, although of course he continued to rule. He had never made remarks by accident. She had asked idly for a painter to make her a landscape of Macau harbor, afterwards, and studied the alteration in the ships thoughtfully. They were indeed larger than in former days, and they seemed to carry many cannon.

Mianning, she knew, felt strongly that they must reach out and lay a heavy calming hand upon the waters which those ships were stirring. He was a young man, of course, with a young man's energy and courage, but it did not follow that he was wrong. Nor was she prepared to dismiss Yongxing's objections to the outrageous behavior of the barbarian merchants smuggling in opium and ignoring the laws of the monarch they courted so assiduously. These were matters for others to resolve, however, not her.

Or had been. She gazed at her eggs again. When the Jiaqing Emperor had asked her to make the attempt, she knew it was not an act without weight. It had not been precisely a decision, yet. After all, someone must come to the throne, and that heir would require a Celestial companion. Prince Mianning was the only plausible companion at present, but many years might go forward without a formal commitment, years during which political opponents might continue to hope for a younger prince to rise in competition.

But it had been very *near* a decision. The Emperor's health was growing uncertain, and his only other son was very young. He had wished to give a mark of support to Mianning, and to smooth the course of a likely succession which might otherwise erupt into the horror of familial strife and even civil war. He did not wish to firmly come down upon one side or another in the central argument, but to send a message that the stability of the state outweighed in importance all other considerations. And she had agreed, sharing that opinion wholeheartedly.

Now, however—there were two eggs. And while the existence of a single Celestial would have imparted a gentle but sure degree of stability to the succession, a second one would undermine it instead. Young Prince Miankai was the only possible companion for the second Celestial at present. He would be elevated to attention far beyond his years, and made a desirable target for every faction and official who hoped to wield influence over the next Emperor. The Emperor would be faced with the very choice he had wished to avoid: either to formally name Mianning his heir, raising him to a strength which would disappoint and inflame his political enemies, or to tacitly permit such maneuvering, even though it would weaken Mianning's position and make Miankai vulnerable.

The Empress came a few days later, and sat with Qian for some time. She was Miankai's mother, but she had overseen Mianning's education as well, and she did not suffer from the lust to see her own son crowned. They listened together to some encouraging music sung for the benefit of the eggs, and sipped tea. "Many cares beset the throne," the Empress said, and after a pause added, "The honorable Prince Yongxing has been most attentive to his young nephew of late."

Qian understood what she was saying. Prince Yongxing could not be easily kept from his nephew. He had disqualified himself for the throne where his brother now sat, by taking Lien's companionship upon himself when she had first hatched rather than seeing her sent away. But in so doing, he had increased his standing at the court to nearly the level of the throne. The Emperor tolerated no slights or even the suggestion of disrespect towards him. He was deeply sensible that his elder brother had removed himself from his path, and subsequently had supported his succession.

Qian paced the pavilion round her eggs in distraction the rest of the afternoon. She understood perfectly the hints and warnings she had been given. Yongxing meant to exert every effort to make Miankai a rival for the throne, and Mianning would not sit quietly while it was done. They would carry out their silent struggle over her eggs; they would not scruple to make every attempt to unhealthily attach one of the hatchlings too early, and to induce the other to reject the other candidate for their affections, feeding them on lies and whispers. The conflict might even take a more horrible form still: what if one side or another, frenzied by the circumstances, attempted harm to one or even both of the eggs? She could not think so ill of either Mianning or of Yongxing themselves, but they had many supporters less honorable than eager.

That fear kept her sleepless several nights in a row, even after she had demanded a doubling of the guards and attendants around her eggs. She could not stop pacing. Chu finally came and offered to keep watch during the night, to let her rest, and she went to the garden and sank into slumber at once, aching with deep exhaustion. In the morning, she roused and came at once to inspect them. Nothing untoward had occurred, but she curled round them at once and nosed them over with great anxiety. Chu said quietly, sitting beside her, "This cannot be healthy for either you or the eggs. The situation must be resolved swiftly."

"In what way can it possibly be resolved?" Qian said wearily. "Save the one which drives my fears."

Chu was silent a while beside her, and then he said finally, "It was once proposed by the illustrious Qianlong Emperor that Lien should be sent away."

Every instinctive feeling rejected the answer at once. But Qian did not need to search long to find an answer which came from better sources. "Lien was a different case. There is no allied ruler upon whom the Emperor can bestow a true Celestial without giving rise to unhealthy and dangerous ambition."

"No allied ruler," Chu agreed, and paused before continuing. "The Emperor has lately received word from the barbarian nation known as France. They have chosen to raise their ruler to the rank of Emperor. He will be crowned in the winter."

He nosed at her gently before he left her again, meant for comfort. Qian curled shivering around her eggs. No one would try to take one of them from her by force, naturally. The Emperor had not even made a suggestion, which might have placed her in the position of having to defy his will. Chu had himself only said a few words in passing. She might as easily close her ears to the hint, and keep them both safe by her. When the eggs had hatched, the Emperor might command one of them to depart, himself.

But she was a Celestial, and not a lesser creature, who might permit her own feelings to come before the needs of the state. She had been the Companion of Heaven. Hongli had trusted her judgement, and he had gone to his rest glad to know she would remain at court, and lend her wisdom and protection to his successors. She would not now betray him with selfishness. Nor would she be so cruel to the growing hatchling. What agony would it be to find yourself exiled to a distant and barbaric land, when you had been hatched amid the glories of the Imperial court? Better never to have known what you had lost. If the egg went now, it would mature with a foreign tongue bathing its shell, and hatch to find itself the honored companion to the highest lord of its adopted land. It would not suffer the anguish of separation, nor the sting of envy.

They came for the egg three days later. She had quietly sent word to the Emperor that she would be interested in meeting the ambassadors of this Emperor-to-be, who had been so greatly favored by Heaven as to rise to so high a seat. He brought them before her in his own person, so great a mark of consideration and kindness that she could not help but feel soothed a little. The ambassadors spoke haltingly and were awkward in their courtesies, but though their manner was rough, they seemed to her sincere; and their astonishment, when the Emperor informed them that he had chosen to send a Celestial egg to their lord as a coronation gift, was satisfyingly enormous: they understood at least a little the magnitude of the honor that was being done them.

The Emperor permitted them their ecstasies of gratitude, and then abruptly summoned the party of attendants who would go with the egg: they had brought a crate lined with silk and wool, all made ready. They gave her no time to worry or think. Qian managed to open her coils long enough to let them come to the eggs, and one of the attendants asked her quietly, "Honored one, may I inquire which egg is the younger?"

Qian hesitated, struggling, and then abruptly she lowered her nose and gestured instead to the first egg, the one that had come forth a few scant minutes earlier; the elder brother, the lucky one. No one would ever know, she told herself, around the thrumming sensation deep in the lower chambers of her throat, as they carefully lifted the egg from its cart and into the safe place waiting to receive it. That tiny measure of good fortune was all the advantage either egg possessed. She could give it nothing more.

They closed the lid upon the crate and carried it out of her sight. Others took away the egg's empty cart at the same time. In moments, there was no trace that a second egg had ever been present. All had been accomplished with enormous speed and deftness. The ambassadors were escorted away, and only the Emperor remained; even her attendants and his own left, sent away, and when they were gone, he bowed to her as he had in the days when she had been his father's companion. "I honor your wisdom, Lady Qian," he said formally.

"I am honored by your kindness, Son of Heaven," she whispered. But she was grateful when he left her alone with her remaining egg. She coiled around the lonely cart and spread her wings sheltering around it and over her head.

Dragons and Decorum

(art by Laurie Damme Gonneville)

Captain E. Bennet of Wollstonecraft

Author's Note: As soon as I saw Laurie Damme Gonneville's illustration, this story leapt into my head almost entirely complete.

"WELL, MR. BENNET, SUCH DREADFUL news," his lady said to him one day. "The Seventh Wing is come to Meryton. Whatever is to be done?"

"I do not see that anything can be done," Mr. Bennet said. "The Admiralty are most unreasonable, to be sure, but I believe they insist on safeguarding the nation. We will have to endure not being bombarded by the French in the night."

"Oh! Pray do not joke about such a thing, and you must know I am speaking of Elizabeth: what is to be done?"

Miss Elizabeth Bennet did not ordinarily occasion any great maternal anxiety. Indeed, Mrs. Bennet contrived tolerably well not to think of her second daughter at all, save to pronounce her "comfortably settled, with her uncle," and very occasionally to write the girl a long, badly-spelt letter detailing the most recent of her woes and nervous maladies. The object of these missives responded with brief and encouraging notes which a more careful reader than her mother might suspect were written without any reference to the original.

Mrs. Bennet was of a family less respectable than her husband's. Her elder brother was indeed an officer in the notorious Aerial Corps, though himself gentlemanlike in his manners and respectably married. Having achieved the rank of first lieutenant, the elder Gardiner did not look further, and as officer to one of the Chequered Nettles stationed in London, enjoyed there a settled family life. They naturally did not move among the better circles of society, and displayed a distressing lack of concern for it.

Meanwhile, with her husband's estate entailed upon a distant cousin, and having produced five daughters dowered with little more than an inclination to be handsome, Mrs. Bennet early began to consider herself justified in indulging an anxiety for their future. Her fretful concerns occasionally found in her brother an audience, and drew him at last to bring forward a hesitant offer couched in vague terms, of a form of support which he might perhaps be able to offer one of his nieces.

Her answering raptures made him cautious. "Pray do not be so enthusiastic, my dear sister," he said with high alarm. "I must speak with my brother, first," and insisted on closeting himself at length with Mr. Bennet without any further intelligence.

"I am sure you have the best uncle in the world," Mrs. Bennet informed her eldest daughters, Jane and Elizabeth then being thirteen and ten years of age respectively, and considered old enough to bear their mother company in the sitting room of a morning when no more entertaining visitors had presented themselves. Her good opinion was a little shaken, shortly thereafter, when Mr. Bennet disclosed to her the full nature of her brother's proposal. But she was possessed of that happy sort of character which was very soon able to discard such considerations as danger and hard use and loss of respectability, when these were weighed against the certain and immediate satisfaction of having one of her beloved children taken off her hands. After only a brief hesitation she renewed her approbation, and pressed her husband to accept.

This was no less than to sacrifice one of her daughters to the Aerial Corps, to be trained as a captain for some peculiar and recalcitrant breed of dragon which refused male handlers. "I would not suggest it for a moment, my dear sister," Lieutenant Gardiner said that evening to his sister and brother-in-law, as they sat together in the drawing-room after dinner, "save that there are two Longwing breeding pairs currently at work and a third to come shortly. We confidently expect to have a new beast to harness every other year for the next decade, and there is a sad lack of coming candidates. My niece is quite certain to make captain, if she have any aptitude for the work."

"Oh! A captain in the Corps!" Mrs. Bennet said. "I am sure it would be a splendid thing for any of the girls."

"And which of the girls would you propose?" Mr. Bennet said, in his dry way, having been silent for most of the evening. Mrs. Bennet was not so unnatural a mother as to be equal to the question.

The next afternoon, the two elder Miss Bennets had the questionable pleasure of accompanying their father and uncle to the covert at

Meryton, where a courier-dragon had brought him on his visit, and of seeing the beast themselves. Jane shrank away in alarm from the inquisitive Winchester, which had thrust its head forward to inspect the ribbons on her gown, but Elizabeth, already independent-minded and bidding fair, in her mother's opinion, to be a difficult girl, after only a few shrinking moments asked if she might safely pet the creature.

"I do not mind at all," the dragon answered her, "—you might scratch my cheek right there beneath the harness; there is an itch I cannot get at conveniently."

Too young to be much surprised at being addressed by a dragon, she industriously squirmed a small hand beneath the leather harness and scratched away heedless of the inch-long fangs near-by, to the dragon's loud appreciation. Her uncle directed a significant glance at her father over her head. Three weeks later she willingly departed under his aegis for the training grounds in Scotland, and so was lost to her parents and to respectable society.

But she had done well in her new profession, and her uncle's promise had lately been fulfilled: since the spring, she had been *Captain* E. Bennet, of the somewhat scandalously named Wollstonecraft, and her last letter to her parents had announced her assignment, with her newly trained dragon, to the Seventh Wing.

"I am surprised, my dear," Mr. Bennet now answered Mrs. Bennet. "I have heard you lament the distance between you and your daughter any time these past nine years. Surely this must be an occasion for rejoicing."

"Of course I am excessively glad to see dear Elizabeth again," Mrs. Bennet said. "But if she is to be in Meryton, she cannot fail to meet the rest of the village in the street from time to time. Whatever will they think? It cannot do the other girls any good."

"You are quite right. We must make our sentiments on the matter perfectly plain. We will give a ball for her in two weeks, and invite the neighborhood."

Mrs. Bennet objected in horror and at length. Mr. Bennet was unmoved. He was of a capricious and sardonic nature, which delighted in human folly. Elizabeth had been his favorite for her quick wit, even as an unformed child, and he had really regretted her loss. His consent to her departure for the Corps had only been obtained, though he had never avowed it, from a peculiar fear of the sorrow which might be her lot if she *did* marry to secure her future, unlike his wife's concern for the reverse.

That same peculiarity in his character now induced him to insist upon an occasion which promised to give pleasure to no-one directly concerned, as Captain Bennet's reaction on receiving the brief note which informed her of the honor to be done her more nearly resembled her mother's than anything else.

"Whatever am I to do?" she demanded of her interested dragon, who was peering over her shoulder at the letter.

Wollstonecraft offered no assistance, merely advising her with great enthusiasm to purchase a dress and jewels. "You are sure to meet a tall and handsome stranger," she added, "who will fall madly in love with you." The dragon had in her first year already developed a great taste for gothic literature, which led her to view an eligible lover as a desirable sort of prize; and had given her a highly inaccurate notion of the usual course of a ball.

"What a strange creature you are," Captain Bennet said, although with a caress of the long and deadly snout beside her which belied her words. "Nothing could be more inconvenient, if it were in the least likely to happen."

"I do not see why not. You are very pretty, all the aviators say so."

Wollstonecraft spoke with immense satisfaction, much to Captain Bennet's mingled mirth and dismay. "They are not thrown much in the way of pretty girls, you know," she answered her dragon, laughing. "I am afraid we cannot consider them reliable authorities."

She could not easily excuse herself from the pleasure of the occasion, not even on the grounds of duty, for the station at Meryton was, she knew very well, a mere way-station where little action was to be expected. She was young, and her dragon even younger, and only necessity had made her a captain and formation-commander with so little experience to her credit. In her rear-officer, Captain Winslow of the Parnassian Vindicatus, she had a twenty-year veteran who was entirely competent to answer any small French incursion without her. The prospects for any larger action were so insignificant as to bar consideration. She could not say it was impossible for her to leave her post for a single night.

Having resigned herself to suffering a ball in her honor, Captain Bennet was not so without vanity that she did not wish to appear to advantage. She was a little better equipped for this task than most young women of the Corps, having been received home at Christmastime, and having besides spent a good deal of time in the society of her uncle's family: one of his own daughters had also gone to the Corps, but the other had preferred to remain in the domestic sphere, and had just lately married a promising young officer. And to provide a more immediate advantage, her sister Jane braved the terrors of the covert to escort her to the town seamstress.

"My dearest Jane," Captain Bennet said, embracing her sister, "How well you look! I must be very glad to have gone to the Corps. I would certainly have required a great deal of fortitude otherwise to be always outshone by my sister. Here, this is my darling Wollstonecraft: is she not lovely?"

"Oh! Yes," Miss Bennet said, trying to smile despite trembling: only a very partial spirit indeed could have applied the epithet to Wollstonecraft, who added to the usual glaring orange eyes of a Longwing a slightly lengthened and vicious-looking snout framed between the yellowed spurs of bone whence the deadly acid came. Her upper teeth protruded around her lower jaw, producing an overhang rather like stalactites, and these were dangerously serrated. "Lizzy, she will not—she will not bite, will she?"

"Of course I will not bite," Wollstonecraft said, "unless a French dragon should try and come this way: and in that case, I should spit, and not bite them, most likely. So you are Elizabeth's sister? I am very pleased to meet you. Pray will you be sure that Elizabeth buys a very nice gown? I am fond of purple, myself, and I think she would look excellently well in it."

Captain Bennet withdrew to her small private cabin to exchange her trousers and coat for a walking dress, and shortly the sisters walked out of the covert and into the town arm in arm. "So tell me more of this Bingley fellow of yours," Captain Bennet said. "All I know from my mother's last letter is he has five thousand a year and danced with you twice at the assembly, and that I am to wish you happy at any moment; and from yours, only that he is somewhere between sixteen and eighty years of age."

"Oh!" Jane cried, coloring a little, "I do wish—I do wish that our mother might express herself with a little more circumspection. Of course she was writing to you, my dear Lizzy, and no one could ask her to be anything less than frank, but I fear she has led you astray. Mr. Bingley has been—is—extremely civil, but nothing more than that."

"Is he handsome?"

"Anyone would call him handsome, I think. His manners are all that is pleasing, and I will say that he is the most charming gentleman of my acquaintance. But that is all."

"Oh, that is all, is it! I see my mother has understated the case, for once," and from this conclusion Elizabeth refused to be moved by her sister's continuing protests. "Unless he is a great fool, he must love you, for he will not find anyone half so beautiful and so good-natured any-where in the world, so if your heart is won, I must count you as good as lost. I can only hope he deserves you, dear Jane."

She thus found herself glad of the ball after all, for its offering her the opportunity of looking Mr. Bingley over more closely. Perhaps as a natural consequence of her now-settled independence, she had begun to think herself a protector of her sisters. Well aware of their mother's single-minded devotion to their establishment, and privately mistrustful of her parent's judgement, she feared to see Jane pressed to enter into a situation which could not give her true happiness.

But on this score she was soon relieved from care. The night of the ball arrived, Mr. Bingley was presented to her early in the evening, and she rejoiced to find him as Jane had described him, an amiable young man with easy and unaffected manners, ready to please and be pleased by his company. "Miss Elizabeth Bennet!" he cried, plainly not even noticing that she had mistakenly shaken his hand, rather than merely giving him her fingers to touch. "I am delighted to make your acquaintance at last. I understand you have been from home long?"

"I have made my home with my uncle these last nine years, sir," Elizabeth said—not untrue, if one considered the Corps their mutual home—"and am only lately settled in Meryton, for a time."

"Well, I am very glad to hear it," Mr. Bingley said, with every appearance of meaning his words. "I know it will not fail to give your sister the greatest pleasure, and I hope we will see a great deal of you, as long as you are here."

His warmth was amply recompensed by the cold bare civility of his sisters. "Your uncle is an aviator, I understand," Miss Caroline Bingley said to Elizabeth, with an air of very faint incredulity, as though she did not care to believe it.

"He is," Elizabeth said, and added with a little pardonable malice, "we have several officers, in our family." She had endured a great deal of hissed whispers from her mother before the party on the need for secrecy, and the deadly danger to her sisters' reputations if her own profession should become known to the company.

She was armored against incivility, however, by the knowledge that a dragon waited eagerly for her to return and give a full accounting of the gowns and jewels worn by every lady present. She did not feel unequal to her company: her gown was silk, her hair had been done up by her mother's maid, and without attaching any great importance to the fact, she was comfortably aware she was in good looks.

She could not help but take a certain small satisfaction in having the young gentlemen of the neighborhood seek an introduction, and solicit her hand in one dance after another. But Captain Bennet was enough her father's daughter to laugh at herself for this vanity, and to be amused rather than piqued when she overheard Mr. Bingley's particular friend, a Mr. Darcy, describe her scornfully to that gentleman as "Tolerable, but not handsome enough to tempt me," when Bingley would have presented him to her as a partner.

Others did not take the remark so lightly, however. "Oh!" Wollstonecraft said, her scarlet eyes widening when this incident had been recounted to her, in the spirit of sharing a joke. "If only I had been there! I should have given him a sharp lesson. *Tolerable*, indeed! My beloved Elizabeth, you must have been the most beautiful lady there, I am sure of it. Although," she added broodingly, "I do wish you had agreed to buy some jewels."

"No, my sister Jane was that," Elizabeth answered, with real satisfaction, "and my family are not rich enough for me to go about buckled in jewels: a fine thing it would look for me to be in diamonds, and my elder sister with a string of pearls."

"Diamonds," Wollstonecraft sighed.

Elizabeth laughed. "I am very content with my ball, in any case. Jane has found herself a charming young man, I believe, who may be the only person in the world as amiable and accommodating as she is herself. They are very well matched. As for Mr. Darcy, I am told by my mother that he is past bearing with, and if she can say so, considering that he has a splendid estate in Derbyshire and ten thousand a year, that paints him a very monster indeed. I can well support the burden of his disapproval."

She thought herself done once more with society, having endured this trial, but events were not to permit her so easy an escape. Having made arrangements to enjoy a country walk with her sister three days hence, Captain Bennet was disturbed to receive a short and ill-written letter from Jane early upon the prescribed morning with her excuses: she was at Netherfield Hall, and too ill to leave the house.

"She must be at death's door to write me such a letter. I think I had better have a look in on her," Elizabeth said to Wollstonecraft. "Will you mind if I have Pulchria lift me over? We cannot go stampeding all Mr. Bingley's game, and the lawn of Netherfield Hall is not large enough for you." This was nearly true, but Elizabeth also thought it ill-advised to take Wollstonecraft anywhere she might encounter the unfortunate Mr. Darcy. The dragon had not ceased to mutter with indignation. "I will come back tomorrow midmorning, at the latest."

"Of course not," Wollstonecraft said, after a moment of visible struggle. "But I will just have a word with Pulchria," she added, "in case you should see that Mr. Darcy," confirming Elizabeth's concern.

Pulchria, a Grey Copper, was one of their rear-wing-dragons, and only six tons; neither she nor her captain had any objection to the short jaunt. Captain Bennet was shortly deposited upon the lawn, and walked up to the house in front of an alarmed audience whose presence was betrayed only by the twitching of curtains in the windows. Thinking not at all of her appearance, she had worn her one other walking-dress, sadly outmoded, and her Hessian boots beneath, which had kicked up a great deal of mud onto her hem by the time she reached the door.

Mr. Bingley received her with great generosity and warmth despite having been called from his breakfast-table by a dragon at the door. The civility of his welcome was not matched by the rest of the scandalized party, who answered her own very perfunctory greetings with a few cold syllables, and as soon as Mr. Bingley escorted her to her sister's room, they were quick to exclaim over her behavior. "Well, Mr. Darcy," Miss Caroline Bingley said to that gentleman, "I am sure you would not wish to see your sister astride a dragon, or presenting such a peculiar appearance."

"Certainly not," Mr. Darcy said, but as his astonishment caused his gaze to follow Captain Bennet as long as she was in sight, this response did not much satisfy Miss Bingley.

Quite unaware of this exchange, Elizabeth was disturbed to find Jane very poorly indeed, and the doctor, who was attending her, unsparing in his concern. "I am afraid I do not know the first thing about nursing, but if you can write me out instructions, I will see it done," she said to that gentleman, and took herself back down to the sitting room, where Mr. Bingley had returned.

"Thank you, sir," she said, in response to his sincere expressions of hope for Miss Bennet's speedy recovery, "but I am afraid Jane is not well at all. However, if you will be so good as to lend me a few of your older maidservants, I trust we may contrive to pull her through the wind."

She addressed Mr. Bingley, unconsciously, with the calm certainty which she was used to use with her own officers and crew. She had been encouraged in that mode early in her training by one of her commanders, Captain St. Germain of Mortiferus. "You're too slight, m'girl," that officer, who suffered not at all from the same complaint, had said, "and too pretty. You shan't be able to bellow the fellows down as Roland or I can do; so you must make it sound there ain't any question they will do as you wish." At first hard-won, by now that assumed air of authority had become second nature in any circumstance where she felt herself in command, and she had not the least hesitation in taking charge of her sister's care even in Mr. Bingley's house.

Mr. Bingley himself did not take notice of her manner: he was too intent upon promising her any assistance she required, and directing his housekeeper to meet her requests at once. But Mr. Darcy regarded her across the room with renewed surprise, and as soon as Elizabeth had gone again, Miss Bingley once more cried out upon her. "What an abominable air of independence!" she said. "I declare I am ready to sink with shame on her behalf. It must be this excessive association with aviators. I would almost say it has destroyed her respectability."

"I think it shows a very great consideration for her sister," Mr. Bingley said, protesting, but he was quickly sunk beneath a storm of opposition from his sisters.

Elizabeth would have returned scorn for scorn, if she had known anything of Miss Bingley's remarks. But she was quite preoccupied, all the rest of the day, with her sister's care. Miss Bennet was far more ill than she had wished to acknowledge even to herself, and her fever proved stubborn enough to hold until early in the evening. The third ice-bath at last broke it, and she was eased into bed weary but with slightly better color.

"There," Elizabeth said, "you begin to look more like yourself, dear Jane. I think we have turned the corner, but I will not leave you until the morning. I hope Wollstonecraft will forgive me, but I am determined to bivouac at the foot of your bed tonight."

"Dearest Lizzy," Jane said drowsily, "I am so very grateful to have you, although I ought not say so, for I know you are neglecting your duty for my sake. But you must go down for dinner."

"I hope not. They cannot want me, and I have nothing to wear."

"You shall wear my clothes. Our mother sent some things for me, when she learned I could not leave directly. Pray do, sister. I cannot be easy in my mind when I have already so abused Mr. Bingley's hospitality."

Reluctantly, Captain Bennet went down in her borrowed gown and slippers, to face a company as unwelcome to her as she was to them. Mr. Bingley she thought better and better of, every moment, but of his sisters and friend she thought less and less. By nature independent-minded, her training and the company of aviators had increased her sense of scorn for condescension and the forms of polite society, when these were unaccompanied by real accomplishment and warmth.

"I hope dear Miss Bennet is better?" Miss Bingley asked her with a thin cold politeness, but as this was followed in close succession by her turning away and pressing Mr. Darcy for his opinion on the ragout of rabbit which had just been offered him, Captain Bennet was very little inclined to view it as evincing any real sentiment.

Her brother's inquiries, when they had retired to the drawing-room, were more eager and more sincere. He repeated several times his hope that Miss Bennet should be wholly well soon, his determination she should not leave one moment sooner than this event, and his pleasure in Elizabeth's own company.

"Thank you, sir," Elizabeth said, touched by his kindness, although she could not feel herself a happy addition to the party. She did not play whist, and had to avow a lack of familiarity with the poets on whom Miss Bingley, with an air of great condescension, inquired for her opinion; and when Mr. Hurst expressed, with a grunt, his dour certainty of Bonaparte's coming across the Channel one of these days, she was unable to refrain from answering with quick scorn, "Not while Mortiferus and Excidium are at Dover."

"Eh? Who?" Mr. Hurst said, and she was recalled to her own indiscretion.

"The Longwings stationed at the covert there," she said as briefly as she might, belatedly conscious she had arrested the attention of all the company.

"You mean the dragons, I suppose," Mr. Bingley said, eager to pursue any line of conversation which should make his guest more comfortable, unaware that she would really have preferred any other. "I am ashamed to say I do not know the first thing about them. Are Longwings very large?"

Elizabeth could not refuse to answer, although she feared to betray herself at any moment. "Middle-weight, sir," she said reluctantly, "but they are vitriolic—they have venom."

"They can't poison all the French coming over," Mr. Hurst said, with a snort.

"A Longwing's venom is capable of working through six inches of oak in ten minutes. A drop will kill a man at once. Bonaparte cannot come across with less than a hundred dragons, if then, so long as we have Longwings on the defense."

Captain Bennet spoke decidedly and with pride. Although she would have been sorry to embarrass Jane, not even that consideration could outweigh her loyalty to the Corps. But she was conscious of putting herself forward, and she took the pause which her response brought as an opportunity to escape to the other side of the room and pretend to be perusing the books on the shelf there.

This brought her nearly to Mr. Darcy's elbow, where that gentleman sat writing a letter, and in a minute Captain Bennet became aware that he had paused in his work and was sitting back in his chair, looking at her as though he meant to address her. She glanced at him with open inquiry, wondering why he did not speak, before she recollected that she ought not have taken notice. But by then he had flushed a little and rose to join her politely, much to her dismay.

"I suppose you are fond of Vauban," he said, naming one of the authors on the shelf she regarded.

"I find he relies too much on mathematics, sir; in my opinion Coehoorn is more useful, as a practical matter," she answered, thoughtfully, before she recollected too-late again that she ought know nothing of fortifications, and supposed that he had been meaning the remark as a jest at her expense.

Mr. Darcy, who had merely cast upon anything to hand on which to make conversation, was unaware of the sentiments he had provoked: he only recognized that her color heightened and her eyes were remarkably brilliant. "I have not made a study of such matters myself," he said, and then was silent.

"I begin to fear you must think us very useless creatures, Miss Elizabeth Bennet," Mr. Bingley called to her from the table. "And I cannot defend myself against the charge, but I assure you Darcy is a very sober fellow—at school he was forever at his books."

"And bent upon studies more natural and appropriate to your station in life," Miss Bingley said to Mr. Darcy, quick to interject herself into the conversation in his defense. "I am sure Miss Elizabeth will agree with me, will you not? After all, we cannot all be aviators."

"By all means," Captain Bennet said, still in a temper, which this sly remark did not improve. "It is not everyone who can occupy themselves with the business of defending the nation."

She was sorry directly she had spoken; if Mr. Darcy and Miss Bingley chose to be uncivil, the same behavior was not pardonable on her part, having imposed herself upon her host. "The management of a great estate must be as difficult as that of dragons," she added hastily, to take the sting from her words, "and as necessary," and offered Darcy a slight inclination of her head, as she would have made to a fellow-officer whom she had accidentally offended.

Darcy answered it in kind, and with Jane as her excuse, Elizabeth shortly made her escape from the drawing-room, feeling an equal share of mortification and disdain. "I must confess to you, dearest Jane," she said, when she sat beside her sister once again, "as wretched as I feel to have so exposed myself to your friends, and on your behalf for having so awkward a sister, I cannot but be profoundly grateful for the good fortune which gave me my escape from a life of such intercourse. How can it be supported! Such idleness, mingled with such insipidity! I should far rather face a volley of rifle-fire than endure many more nights of like company."

WITH JANE on the mend, Elizabeth had intended to return to the covert at the first hour of the next morning, but this aim was frustrated, when she woke, by a cold rain falling. She did not think the conditions so very bad; she would have set forth glad only for the loan of a cloak, and spoke of asking, but Jane expressed so much astonishment at the idea of her walking a few miles in spring rain that Elizabeth was forced to realize she would cut an even more peculiar figure with her company if she were to insist upon leaving the house straightaway.

"I must send a word to the covert, then," she said, giving it up, and scribbled a few hasty lines to be read to Wollstonecraft. She enclosed the letter to Captain Winslow, and carrying it downstairs looked for a servant to take it—a great nonsense, she thought, that any domestic might be sent to Meryton with a note, and she forced to remain indoors, as though she would dissolve in a mild shower for having been born a gentleman's daughter.

She encountered Miss Bingley downstairs and stopped briefly to assure that lady of her sister's improving health. "We will of course take ourselves out of your way at the first opportunity," Captain Bennet said. "You must long be wishing your house to yourselves, and I am sorry the rain must keep us here."

Miss Bingley said all that was polite and necessary, with no great enthusiasm, and glancing at the letter said, "May I be of service, Miss Elizabeth? You are writing to your uncle, I suppose?"

"No, my uncle is gone to London," Elizabeth said. "But I should be obliged to you if someone might take this letter to Meryton, for Captain Winslow."

Miss Bingley looked briefly as astonished as if Elizabeth had asked for the moon and then with wooden face put out her hand and said, "If you please."

Elizabeth wondered a little, but thinking little of Miss Bingley's sense, and caring less for her opinions, she did not investigate her reaction; she merely handed over the note, and returned to Jane's room to bear her company and chivvy her into swallowing a little more broth and bread.

Jane was so much improved that by the noon hour, she was able to rise and dress. Elizabeth saw her escorted downstairs, and sheltered from draughts in a place by the fire in the drawing-room. The rest of the company joined them shortly thereafter, with sidelong glances at Elizabeth which she did not understand. "My dear Miss Bennet," Miss Bingley said to Jane, "how happy I am to see you so much better. We must have a private word, if the rest of the company can permit it."

Elizabeth could hardly ignore so forceful a hint; she took herself to the other side of the room, relieved to be pursued only by Mr. Bingley, who also bore a curiously anxious look, but spoke to her civilly, until Jane raised her voice from the fire and said, "Lizzy, pray, is this your letter?"

"Good God!" Elizabeth cried, seeing the note in Jane's hand, "Miss Bingley, I depended upon you to have it sent. They will have missed me at the covert this hour and more."

"If you do not scruple to acknowledge it," Miss Bingley said, rising from her chair with color in her cheeks, "I shall not to say that I wonder at your effrontery in attempting to make me your accomplice. As a guest in this house, you ask me to send an illicit letter for you to a gentleman unconnected with you in any way—"

"Impertinent nonsense," Elizabeth said sharply, and turning to Mr. Bingley, "Sir, you must get your cattle in the stables at once, and tied, if you do not want them to spook: there will be a dragon here for me at any moment."

"A dragon for you?" Mr. Bingley said, in plaintive confusion, but Elizabeth was already hurrying for the door, and stopped only long enough to turn back and kiss Jane's cheek, and beg her to forgive the abrupt desertion.

Mr. Darcy, standing by the door, followed her into the corridor with a sharp frown on his face. "Miss Bennet!" he said, and when she paid him no attention and continued towards the front of the house, he caught up to her quick strides. "I cannot understand your behavior," he said, "—it admits of no respectable characterization. At the very least, you owe your host an explanation."

"What I owe my host," Elizabeth said, without slackening her pace, "is to keep his house from being torn down about his ears—oh, damn and blast it all, there she is."

They had come into the gallery, and with the rain slackening and the clouds thinning, Wollstonecraft's shadow showed dark on the grounds outside, the enormous outspread wings throwing a rapidly increasing blot. Elizabeth gave over trying to find her way to a door and instead dashed to the nearest large window. Climbing awkwardly to the sill, she managed to unhook the two heavy panes and throw them open to the air, while Mr. Darcy stared up at her with astonishment.

"Wollstonecraft!" Elizabeth called, waving a hand madly and with impatience thrust away Darcy's arm: he had climbed up beside her and was trying to restrain her, and for a moment she thought she would have to knock him down. Wollstonecraft's answering roar shook all the panes as she descended on the grounds and thrust her head towards the window.

"Elizabeth, Elizabeth," she said, "—you did not come! You are quite well? You are not hurt?" She twisted her head to present one enormous and coldly slitted orange eye to Darcy, who to his credit did not immediately flee the scene, but stood with his arm still outthrust to shield Elizabeth from the jaws before her, although his face had gone pale. "Who is that gentleman? Have they kept you here?"

"No, no, my dear!" Elizabeth said hurriedly, "I wrote you a letter, only it went astray: pray don't be alarmed. We must be back to the covert at once, though. Do give me your leg to get up."

Wollstonecraft drew her head away from the window with a low grumble of dissatisfaction. "As long as you are with me again, and you are quite well." She put out her foreleg to let Elizabeth climb out of the window and into her grasp, making a protective cage of her talons. "Is that Mr. Darcy?" she added, suspiciously.

"That is quite enough: I cannot have you snap at him," Elizabeth said, with alarm.

"I will not *snap*, but before I go away, he *shall* say that you are not merely tolerable: and that he is very sorry to have been so ungentlemanly and rude."

She swung her heavy head back towards the open window; Mr. Darcy, still fixed upon the sill, stared up at the cold look bent upon him, at first only bewildered by such a reproof, coming from such a corner; then he understood the words and flushed deeply. He said awkwardly, "I beg your pardon, Miss Bennet—"

"*Captain* Bennet," Wollstonecraft hissed, angrily.

"Pray will you be silent, you miserable creature," Elizabeth said despairingly. "You will have us in the soup directly. Mr. Darcy, I beg your pardon for her abominable manners, and hope that you will pay no attention to her; she is in a temper and does not know what she is saying. We must go! Pray make my apologies; good-bye."

She kicked Wollstonecraft as hard as the slippers would allow, and with a final grumble the dragon withdrew from the house and took herself back aloft. "Well," Elizabeth said aloud to herself in consolation, as the wind tore at her thin and useless gown, which she was sorry to take away with her in exchange for a pair of good boots and a sensible dress, "at least I will never have to look him in the face again."

ALTHOUGH THE name Pemberley had a vaguely familiar ring, Elizabeth was too weary, after the dreadful defeat and the long flight from London, to search her memory; she wanted only to put Wollstonecraft down somewhere, and get her formation some sort of fodder to share out for the night. The couriers were flying between the retreating formations with assignments: they were each of them assigned to one large estate or another, and granted liberty to hunt deer.

They landed upon a broad and beautiful green sward, in the last hours before sunset. Vindicatus laid down the four cannon he carried with a deep sigh of relief; the middle-weights and light-weights set down their two or one apiece, and Elizabeth slid from Wollstonecraft's back with only a silent pat to her neck. The crews busied themselves creating some kind of order out of the general confusion, and Elizabeth nodded to Rowling, her ground-crew master, who told off a few men to the great house high up on the hill, for supplies.

"Do you think you could hunt for everyone, my dear Wollstone-craft?" she asked, low: she hated to ask for more, after Wollstonecraft had been aloft all day, but she alone of the dragons in their company had not been burdened with cannon, kept free to maneuver in case the French beasts should catch them. They had been detailed off by Admiral Roland to cover the Corps' retreat.

"Of course," Wollstonecraft said stoutly, and took herself into the forest; in a little while she came back with five limp deer, and all the dragons tore into the lean frames without any hesitation. "I have eaten another," Wollstonecraft said, licking her chops clean of blood, "and there is a lake just over the hill when we are thirsty: and oh! Elizabeth! The loveliest house imaginable."

"I will go and have a look, Winslow, if you have no objection," Elizabeth said, wanting badly to wash her face, and when she had gone up and rinsed her mouth and spat, she took off her flying hood and patted down her blown hair. She looked across the water, tiredly, at the great golden expanse of Pemberley House standing there, as wide across as the lake itself. It seemed to her almost dreamlike after the fury and struggle of the day. And as she stood there, the master of the house came out of the wood around the edge of the lake, walking swiftly towards the encampment, and halted when he saw her.

Captain Bennet stared at him blankly and said without thinking, "Mr. Darcy!"

"Miss Bennet," he said, in equally instinctive answer, then stared at her. She was in flying-gear, of course: trousers, Hessians, her long leather coat with the split tails and her sword and muskets belted at her hip.

"Were you coming to the camp?" she said after a moment. "We can walk down together."

He fell into step with her, silenced momentarily by the very number of questions provoked by her appearance. He had not forgotten Miss Elizabeth Bennet in the intervening three years, and indeed had long wished to see her again, and to demand of her some rational, if not respectable, explanation for the incident which she had caused at Netherfield House.

He knew that the elder Miss Bennet had confided some explanation to Mr. Bingley in apology for the scene which had been visited upon his house, and the confusion of his stables. But Bingley refused to communicate that explanation, having received it in confidence; he could only say he was himself perfectly satisfied, and that Miss Elizabeth Bennet had acted as she ought. Yet his character was sufficiently complaisant and generous to have made Darcy doubt this conclusion exceedingly, and to continue to desire a confrontation with the guilty party.

He knew he was to blame for having so enthusiastically pursued the society of the Bennets, in seeking that confrontation, that he had neglected to preserve his friend from the danger of that same society. Darcy had gone to half a dozen assemblies and house parties where Miss Elizabeth Bennet might have been expected to appear. Finding her gone on one excuse after another, he had brooded on her absence without attention for the progression of Bingley's courtship. When Darcy had finally been roused to alarm, Bingley, emboldened by Miss Jane Bennet's confidence, had already persuaded himself of his place in that lady's affections, and he refused to be moved therefrom by all the entreaties which Darcy and his sisters could make. Darcy could afterwards only console himself for this failure by considering that the lady was as admirable in every other regard excepting her connections as she was lamentable in those, and that the match was already proving a remarkably happy one.

But the Seventh Wing had departed for Edinburgh even before the wedding, and in so doing had put an end to all hope of further intercourse between Mr. Darcy and Miss Elizabeth Bennet. Not, however, an end to his thoughts of her. The mode of her departure from Netherfield House might have been sufficient to fix her in his memory as a figure of scandal, but without his wishing it so, another feeling also had secured her place as a woman of whom he had not ceased to think, and against whom he found himself comparing all others of his acquaintance.

From time to time, against his will, he recalled as plainly as though he stood there in the gallery again her slim figure standing upon the broad window-sill, heedless of the rain and wind which billowed the thin gown against her body and tore her hair loose—recalled her arm outstretched to calm the savage beast bending towards her, and felt her once more slip away from beneath his grasp as she stepped into its talons. He had struggled again and again to conquer the unruly sentiment which made so disreputable a scene nevertheless impossible to forget, without success.

He had tried to persuade himself that he was shocked, more than any other emotion; when this effort failed him, he settled it with himself that he only acknowledged her courage, as one might admire a worthy foe—he had struggled himself not to be unmanned in the face of the dragon. But he looked at her again now in the twilight, and before they reached the camp he halted and said abruptly, "Miss Bennet!"

She looked at him with some apprehension. He said, "Forgive me—I would speak as the friend of your brother Mr. Bingley, as he is not here; I hope you know that any protection I may offer you, on his behalf, I would be honored to do. I hope you will come to the house and stay with us as long as you wish. My sister is presently at home with her companion, a widow of respectable character, and I will take the liberty to extend her invitation with my own."

We may well be astonished at such a leap from condemnation to welcome, if we disregard the power of Mrs. Bingley's assurances, Bingley's own certainty, and an as-yet unnamed feeling in Mr. Darcy's breast, which had joined forces to defend Elizabeth's character in his mind. He knew enough, more than he wished, of Mrs. Bennet, and recalling her want of scruple began to wonder if perhaps her vulgar determination to see her daughters settled had sacrificed Elizabeth to some evil position. What this might rationally be, he could not conceive, but his suspicions were formed by dimly remembered fairy-stories of childhood, in which dragons figured as the devourers and gaolers of innocent maidens.

Elizabeth was entirely unaware of the direction of his thoughts. Having fled his society in lively dread of the consequences of having betrayed the respectability of her family, she had never considered that a brief exchange during a rainstorm, with a hissing dragon for accompaniment, might not have conveyed to Mr. Darcy a full and accurate understanding of her circumstances and her role in the Corps. She answered him therefore without any of that ordinary caution which she might have used to conceal her position, from one she did not think aware of it. "I am very sensible of the kindness of your invitation, Mr. Darcy—I beg your pardon most sincerely that I must refuse. I cannot leave Wollstonecraft or my men out in the cold."

"Your men?" Mr. Darcy said, but they had reached the camp, where a fresh courier had landed, and Captain Winslow turning addressed Elizabeth and said, "Dispatches, Captain Bennet," as he gave them to her.

"Thank you, Captain Winslow," she said, and broke the seal to read them quickly. "Gentlemen, the scouts have swept the countryside behind us, and it is confirmed that Marshal Davout has fallen off our tails," she said, to the general nods and relief of her formation-captains, who had gathered close around her to hear the news. "The Corps is falling back on Kinloch Laggan. Our orders are to hold here for the moment as a rear position, and secure our own supply as best we can."

She gave a few further orders to that end, and then turned to Mr. Darcy, whose stares she once more misunderstood. "Mr. Darcy," she said, "will you be so good as to walk with me a moment," and taking his arm guided him back out of earshot. He yielded to the pressure of her hand, made unresisting by surprise. She saw that surprise, but misjudged its source. "You must be wondering, sir," she said soberly, "and I shall not attempt to conceal the evil news; there can be no hope of doing so for long. The worst you can imagine is true—Dover is lost—London lost."

Although Elizabeth had misunderstood his looks, her news repaired her mistake: Mr. Darcy was not of a character to dwell upon his own confusion, when he had just received intelligence of so staggering a blow to his nation; all his questions were forgot at once, and he cried, "Good God!" in real horror.

Elizabeth shared that horror. She had lately been stationed with Wollstonecraft on the northern coast, an isolated posting she knew very well she had brought on herself by speaking too frankly to the Admiralty of her sentiments at the recent demotion of Admiral Roland. A frantic courier-message had brought them to the battle of the Channel too late to do more than bear witness to its conclusion: fifty thousand men already landed with a hundred French dragons circling for cover above them; and she was now fresh from the newest disaster outside London, where Napoleon had nearly snapped his jaws shut about the entire British Army.

Her spirits were badly bruised, but she was conscious of her duty not to spread demoralizing sentiments; with an effort she rallied herself to add, "I am sorry indeed to be the bearer of such news, but I will leaven it, if I may, by assuring you that hope is not lost; our forces have by and large escaped Bonaparte's trap, and when we have regrouped, I have every confidence in our eventual victory. Which indeed," she added, with a burst of resentment she could not contain, "might not have been so dreadfully forestalled, if only Admiral Roland's advice had been heeded—but I must say no more. I fear, sir, that we have put you out."

"As if any such concern should weigh with you, under these circumstances. You shall have everything it is in my power to provide; and I renew my offer, Miss—Captain Bennet," Darcy corrected himself, not without an involuntary questioning note, which no power could have repressed entirely, "not merely for yourself but of course your—your officers, to quarter with me; I am certain shelter may be contrived for all your men."

"I am afraid the greater difficulty will be in feeding the dragons," Elizabeth said, as they came through the trees around the lake, and found Wollstonecraft sitting raptly on the shore with Pulchria and Astutatis, one of their Yellow Reapers, all of them gazing across the water at the enormous house with all its windows lit up brilliantly, the warm stone capturing the last rays of the sun and shining against the deepening twilight behind it.

"Oh! Elizabeth!" the dragon said, swinging her head about. "Come and look with me. Have you ever seen anything so beautiful? It might all be made of gold. What is that place?"

Mr. Darcy had long nursed, along with his memories of Elizabeth, a painful consciousness of what he considered the failure of his courage, when last confronted with a dragon. He had indeed deliberately come out to greet the aviators on this occasion from an intention to allow himself no such weakness, and was doubly glad in front of Miss Bennet to find himself equal to answering the monstrous creature, "That is my house, Pemberley."

Wollstonecraft rolled one fiery orange eye towards him and exclaimed, "Why, that is Mr. Darcy," followed in a moment by, "Your house?" in tones of rising astonishment.

•———•

"ELIZABETH," WOLLSTONECRAFT said, a week later, "I have thought it over at great length, and I suppose I had better forgive Mr. Darcy after all."

"I should hope so," Elizabeth said. She had been surprised and gratefully so by the welcome which Darcy had extended to their formation: she had not looked for anything but the most unwilling and reluctant cooperation from any landowner on whom they had been summarily imposed, and from Darcy in particular would have expected every effort to avoid intercourse with the scandalous aviators settled upon his grounds. Instead he had thrown wide his house to all of them: he had even presented Elizabeth to his own sister, despite any attempts on her part to demur. "I beg your pardon, Mr. Darcy," she had said, "but I cannot get myself up in a dress when at any moment we may have to go aloft."

"Captain Bennet," he said, "I assure you that my sister will not censure your attire; no one could, when you wear it in the course of your duty."

Elizabeth had been moved although unpersuaded, recalling Miss Bingley's refinements upon Georgiana Darcy's perfect deportment and exquisite manners. However, she could not refuse when so pressed, and the introduction being accomplished, had soon understood that Miss Darcy was taken aback only by painful shyness, and was in any case too much in awe of her older brother to disapprove of anyone whom he presented to her.

"Do you really ride a dragon?" Georgiana had dared to ask her, in little more than a whisper.

"There is nothing more delightful, if you have a head for it, and are dressed for the heights," Elizabeth had said, already easy enough with her company to be incautious, and added without thinking, "I should be happy to take you up of a morning, if you like, once the scouts have reported the roads clear."

Almost at once she had recalled to herself the unsuitability of this suggestion. But even to this Mr. Darcy had not objected. He had given her officers dinner every night, and she had been astonished to find him so affable and warm a host with them as to make all his guests easy, even though as aviators they were nearly all of them unaccustomed to polite society and a table of the sort which he laid before them. He had not blinked to be addressed from five seats away, nor when the officers had handed around the dishes among themselves, while his unhappy footmen tried without success to dart in between and recapture them.

Most vitally, he had laid out from his own stores the oats that necessity now prescribed for the dragons' meals, and had insisted they make free not only of his deer but his handsome herd of cattle. He had made a point of coming to the covert daily to hear the reports of the scouts, and to share what intelligence his own servants and tenants had brought him of the surrounding countryside. By his correspondence with other men of property, of his and his late father's acquaintance, he had even arranged similar assistance for a half-dozen other formation companies and some two dozen couriers, to the material assistance of their communications and spying upon the French operations.

"I should hope so," Elizabeth went on now, "when he has been so invaluable to us: I could wish some gentlemen of the Admiralty would behave half as well as he has." She thought with approval of Darcy's visit that morning; they had walked together through the covert, and he had spoken in a sensible way to Vindicatus, whose massive size might pardonably have given pause to any person not accustomed to dragons.

"I have flown over all his grounds, now, when we have not been patrolling," Wollstonecraft said, "and they are delightful in every particular. Do you know, Elizabeth, there is a ruined castle here, which I have been informed dates to the ninth century and is rumored to contain buried treasure, and atop that rise to the north where that little cage sits," meaning by this an elegant folly large enough to entertain a party of six, "you will find a charming plaza built entirely of Italian marble, ideal for sunning oneself: it has a magnificent prospect over the entire countryside. As for the house, nothing more could be asked: if only I might go inside! But really I cannot imagine there is anything within to compare to the pleasure of looking upon it from without. I should not tire of the sight all my days. And I believe you once said he has ten thousand a year?"

"You mercenary creature. Are these the qualities which have won him your pardon?"

"Well, it is hard to imagine him such a paltry fellow, when he has so many beautiful things, and he has behaved so prettily since we came, that I am willing to grant he has learned his lesson. Perhaps he was only ill, when he spoke so slightingly of you before; he may have had some trouble with his eyesight at the time."

Elizabeth only hummed idly in answer; she was preoccupied with her reports, which indicated that the French foragers were making grievous depredations against the countryside to the south, and so thought nothing more of this conversation; to her regret. For on the next occasion which offered, several days later, when Mr. Darcy had come to the covert to bring them several handsome bullocks from his herd, Wollstonecraft cornered the gentleman and demanded if this were not indeed the case.

"Wollstonecraft!" Elizabeth said, despairingly. "What Mr. Darcy will think of you,"—of us, she privately thought, with a dismay sharper than she would have liked.

But Darcy stammeringly said, "I cannot claim to have been ill at the time, madam; only gravely mistaken, for it is some time since I have considered Captain Bennet one of the handsomest women of my acquaintance," and having delivered this astonishing speech, he at once colored, then bowed and very abruptly departed, leaving behind a deeply satisfied dragon and a deeply distressed captain, who said to the former, "Oh, for Heaven's sake, Wollstonecraft, pray stop prancing. Can you not see this is the most dreadful situation imaginable?"

CAPTAIN BENNET would have been glad to forget the incident entirely; that being beyond her power, she would have been satisfied only to pretend that it had never happened. She was not insensible to the compliment of Mr. Darcy's admiration, nor could she fail, with such explicit proofs made her, to see that admiration working in all his exertions on behalf of herself and her formation. That it must have overcome all the sentiments which had, she knew, opposed him to his friend Bingley's match with Jane, and to any close association with aviators, was only a further testament to its extent.

If her own feelings towards Mr. Darcy had remained unchanged, she might have been little troubled by knowing of his. But those feelings were wholly altered: disdain become respect, dislike become affection. She had come to consider him a man to be relied upon, and one whose company brought her pleasure. And she could not help but recognize that she had indulged in that pleasure, with the excuse of their circumstances, far past the bounds of propriety. Mr. Darcy had called upon her every day; she had welcomed his visits and encouraged them. She had been often alone in his company. He was not a fellow-officer, and their intercourse could not be defended as a matter of duty. It had only seemed so impossible that Mr. Darcy should love her, that she had never considered whether her behavior might be giving rise to sentiments which could never be answered.

"I do not see why not," Wollstonecraft said, maddeningly. "Only think, Elizabeth, how splendid it should be to have you the mistress of Pemberley!"

"And what use do you suppose I should be to Pemberley or its master, when the Corps must send us to London, or station us in Dover after God willing we have chased Napoleon off our shores?" Elizabeth said. "Besides, you absurd creature, he may have fallen in love with me, but he cannot mean to marry me; I am a serving-officer, not a respectable gentlewoman." She had never before counted her reputation any real cost. She still did not really regret it now, but was conscious of a faint pang which served to make her wary of her own feelings. It must be for the best that Mr. Darcy would never propose to her. She could only have given pain, in making him a necessary refusal. She hoped that he would say no more, and resolved to avoid being alone in his company henceforth, and to delegate to her officers the necessary discourse between the covert and the house.

These hopes were frustrated, the next day, when walking to the lakeshore after the morning's patrol, as had become her custom, she accidentally encountered Mr. Darcy lingering in a small copse of trees along the path. She hesitated, and nearly turned back; but he caught sight of her and coming near held out a folded and sealed letter, which she received on instinct. "Captain Bennet, I hope you will do me the favor of reading that letter," he said, and bowing took his leave.

Elizabeth wanted almost nothing less than to read the letter; she carried it back to her small bivouac as gingerly as an incendiary, and considered whether it ought not be put on the fire at once. But curiosity was too strong to be overcome. She opened the envelope and read, in a clear strong hand,

> Captain Bennet:
> I beg you not to fear, on opening this letter, that it should contain the further expression of sentiments, which if not grossly offensive, could nevertheless offer you neither pleasure nor satisfaction. The demands of honor alone could justify laying this missive before you, and it has been formed in no expectation of any reward save the comfort of having made a deserved apology to one on whom, I fear, I have inexcusably encroached. While I hardly claim to be owed your attention, I do sincerely request it, and hope that you will grant it from generosity of spirit.

That my behavior towards you has been such as to raise expectations in the eyes of the world, if not in your own breast, I have been unpardonably late to recognize. The dreadful circumstances attendant on your arrival at Pemberley, which must have been your own foremost concern, I cannot claim as an excuse. Indeed, the fear that you may have been impelled by a sense of duty to endure unwanted attentions has formed no small part of my anxiety to deliver this letter to you. If this be the case, I must beg your pardon, while offering you my assurances that these shall never be renewed, and that those small efforts on my part which have only been my due, not to you but to our nation and our King, shall not slacken as a consequence.

My sense of your own character, however, and of your forthrightness and courage, has leavened this particular fear. I trust I have not been so insensible as to force my company upon you unwilling, and still more do I trust that you would have acted swiftly, had I indeed made myself disgusting to you. Yet this should not render me blameless—indeed, the opposite. The charge that I had attempted to insinuate myself into the affections of a lady the close connection of my nearest friend, and forced to remain in my sphere by the exigencies of war, should hardly be leavened by my having succeeded in that indefensible object.

Nor can I pretend to have given no thought to the obstacles which my family and position should lay in the way of my making the only honorable answer to having so grossly trespassed upon your feelings, should I have done so. You know too well, I think, that I was at pains to detach my friend Bingley from your sister. That want of connection, and the considerations of propriety, which he wisely refused to regard as an obstacle to his achieving the hand and heart of a lady worth winning, weighed too long and too heavily upon me. I have lately had cause to regret my folly in this regard, seeing in their happy union that best and most desirable outcome which any man might hope for. —Or envy.

Only when I had exposed my feelings to you so outrageously, yesterday afternoon, was I forced to set aside the last of my selfish concerns. It seemed to me then that I had nothing more to do but decide upon the mode of a declaration whose substance was demanded by my honor. I am ashamed to say that it was only in attempting to form that declaration in accordance with the respect I feel for you, that I discovered the impossibility of doing so.

In my self-centered preoccupation, I had neglected to contemplate those obstacles which your position should place before your receiving with pleasure the addresses of any gentleman. Having at last done so, I was struck with their inescapable force. That you should desert your dragon in the hour of our country's need, or worse yet remove her from the fray, must be unimaginable, an act very near treason, and even to propose that you should do so an insult which no person of spirit could easily endure.

I am well aware this explanation is a paltry one. It is little defense to say that pride and vanity have been my distraction. If I had sooner shown the proper consideration for your situation, I should not now find myself obliged to choose how to offend one whom I both esteem and admire. I can only say that I may justly be reproached for anything but a lack of sincere feeling. My folly has not been self-interested, and I hope I have injured no-one worse than myself in its commission. Only one answer can be made, and that is to assure you that if by any act now or henceforth I may make amends for my behavior, I shall be yours to command. I have nothing more to say but God bless you, and to hope you will pardon me for styling myself,

Your Most Obedient Servant,

FITZWILLIAM DARCY

⁕———⁕

CAPTAIN BENNET hardly knew what to make of her letter. That Mr. Darcy should have so far overcome his pride as to wish to pay his addresses to her, in spite of the material objections to the match which she herself had viewed as an impassable bar, would alone have surprised her; that he should have refrained not for the sake of his reputation but for that of her own honor as an officer, was so astonishing as to nearly make her doubt her own understanding. The letter had to be read again. But the meaning did not alter on a second reading, or a third, except for the more inconceivable. Indeed Mr. Darcy had contrived, while not soliciting her hand, to offer his own; the conclusion could be understood in no other way.

It now remained only for Elizabeth to be gratified that she had inspired so fervent an emotion, and to be sorry for the pain she had unintentionally given. These must be the boundaries of her own feelings on the matter. Anything else was impossible. She knew it well. If she read the letter three times more, and folded it away into the inner pocket of her coat rather than burn it, that was only a gesture of sympathy. Her mind dwelt on particular phrases only to extract their full meaning—a small vanity, nothing more. *One whom I both esteem and admire*—there was an encomium indeed! Only the most insensible creature in the world could read those words without a stirring of emotion.

Elizabeth found she must stop herself from bringing the letter out again. "This will not do," she said, and took out her dispatches from that morning, instead. But her mind refused to manage the ciphers properly, still bent upon the puzzle of another text. "I will go flying," she said.

Wollstonecraft was nothing loath to accommodate her wish, but when they were once in the air, insisted on speaking to Captain Bennet only of the many beautiful features of the grounds and the good qualities of their master, all unaware of the pain she was giving. "There is that tower I believe I mentioned to you," she added. "Mr. Darcy tells me it is a hunting lodge: I believe it is larger than many another person's house. Look, there he is; we will go and say good-morning."

Too late Elizabeth reached for the speaking-trumpet: Wollstonecraft had already banked deeply left, descending in a rushing wind that blew away Elizabeth's shout of protest. Mr. Darcy was indeed not far from the hunting-lodge, riding alone. He and his alarmed horse looked up at the same time, and the poor beast bolted out from under him.

"Whyever did it run?" Wollstonecraft said, aggrieved, looking after the horse. "I did not mean to eat it; and if I *had* meant to eat it, I could certainly catch it, whether it ran away from me or no."

"You ought to know by now a horse will run when you come down behind it; that is not a cavalry-mount, with a hood and blinders. Mr. Darcy! Are you very hurt?" Elizabeth called down anxiously, unlatching her carabiners, and slid down Wollstonecraft's side to find that gentleman dazed and with the breath knocked out of him, and a badly wrenched knee.

"I can do very well, Captain Bennet," he said in a voice sufficiently thin of air to belie his words, and tried to stand.

"You cannot at all," Elizabeth said, bracing him just in time to prevent a collapse: the leg did not wish to bear his weight. "Whatever were you thinking?" she said to Wollstonecraft. "We must get him inside the house."

"I am sure that need be no great difficulty," Wollstonecraft said, and with her talons pried open the large front door for them, leaving the iron locks hanging from the torn door-frame. "Now it is open. Here, I will put him inside."

Mr. Darcy submitted with more courage than grace to being gathered up in a Longwing's talons. When Wollstonecraft had deposited him more or less intact upon the floor of his entrance hall and Elizabeth had joined him there, with her help he levered himself onto a sofa draped with holland covers in the parlor just off the hall, and then said, "Thank you, Captain Bennet; if you will send word to the house when you have gone back to the covert, I would be grateful."

Elizabeth struggled with the natural instinct to accept this hint, and thereby put a period to a scene which could only be full of awkwardness; but guilt and practicality restrained her. "I cannot desert you in this state when we have been the cause of your injury," she said, and returning to the doorway called to Wollstonecraft to fly back to the covert, and send for help. She turned back into the parlor reluctantly. Mr. Darcy had stretched out his injured leg, bracing the knee, and he had fixed his gaze resolutely upon the fine prospect outside the window, with a degree of attention better merited if a troop of Bonaparte's soldiers had been crossing the lawn.

They neither of them spoke, until the silence had been prolonged beyond any reasonable duration between two people who had neither of them any occupation, and Elizabeth's sense of the ridiculous came slowly to her rescue. "Mr. Darcy!" she said at last. "I suppose we could not have found ourselves in a more awkward situation. We must consider it an opportunity to display our characters. I fear to expose my own as wretchedly forward, but I will venture to speak. I hope you will permit me to thank you for the letter you gave me."

Darcy did not look at her all at once, but turned his head in such a way as to direct his gaze near her feet, and then lifted his eyes in one swift movement to her face, as though fearing what expression he should encounter. But Captain Bennet only smiled, or tried to, although conscious more than ever that her feelings were far from what they ought to have been. Darcy's reserve was not equal to concealing his suffering, given this much leave to express it; his looks betrayed him, and she could not see his unhappiness without wishing almost to share it.

"The only thanks which ought pass between us," he said, nearly inaudibly, "must be mine, if you should accept my apologies."

"None are necessary. I beg you not to repine any further. My situation is so peculiar, so unworldly one might even say, that even the most refined sense of decorum might fail as a guide. I am very sensible of the consideration that you have shown for my honor, and sorry that my own caution should have failed me. It is so many years since I gave over all thoughts of marriage, and in comparison to the unsettled situation of my sisters, and the burden of our mother's hopes, I little regretted it then."

"*Then?*" Mr. Darcy cried, with a meaningful emphasis upon the word.

Elizabeth colored and was silent. It was now her turn to feel she had betrayed herself. To give Mr. Darcy encouragement, when she could give him no hope, was cruelty; to permit herself to desire what must be forever beyond her reach an indulgence she could not afford. But alas! these rational conclusions did as much good to stem the tide of passion as might be expected from the usual efficacy of such measures.

"Captain Bennet," Darcy said, "—Elizabeth," and struggled to his feet, only to nearly overbalance himself again. She went swiftly to him. His arm leaned across her shoulders; her hands were pressed to his side, bearing up his weight. They looked into one another's faces.

Darcy's restraint failed him. "Elizabeth, will you—"

"I cannot," she said, cutting him short. A calm clarity, heretofore only experienced in the moments directly before battle, had settled upon her. Her own choice was made; now honor demanded she make plain the limits of what she might offer him. "I cannot marry you."

Darcy flinched and would have drawn away. Elizabeth reached her hand for his cheek and turned him back, and deliberately raised her chin. He trembled against her in understanding. For one moment longer he lifted up his eyes, gazing blindly towards the window; then he closed them, and bent his head to meet her lips.

CAPTAIN BENNET returned to the covert late that afternoon in great disorder of spirit. She had known that the Corps might one day ask her to sacrifice her virtue, in hopes of producing an heir to her captaincy; and she had been bluntly and forthrightly educated on the practicalities by Captain St. Germain. "And I won't tell you not to in the meantime," that officer had added, "because that is of no use; this ain't a nunnery we are living in. Only be cautious about it, and never take one of your own officers to bed."

None of this excellent advice had prepared Elizabeth for the particular evils of her present situation. She had accepted with calm resignation the loss of her reputation and the approval of the world; she had long known she would receive no respectable offers of marriage, and hoped only for an amiable, gentlemanlike arrangement with a fellow-officer, when the time came. But these sacrifices she had learned not to regret. That a gentleman had wished despite every barrier between them to bestow upon her hand and heart, and that she should suffer at refusing him, was a grief for which she had never looked.

"And to such an offer!" she cried to herself, alone in her small tent and looking once again through tears at the fatal letter, "—to such a gesture, I have offered in return only the lowest, most vulgar expression of feeling; in exchange for the honor he has done me, I have only stained his, with no hope of ever repairing the spot. What have either of us gained by it, but uneasiness and worse regrets? And yet, when this is all I may ever have of him—"

Reflection did not ease either Captain Bennet's pain or her guilty conscience. She passed an uneasy night, wondering alternately when next she would have the power of being alone with Mr. Darcy, and hoping for the strength of will to avoid another such encounter; she slept only fitfully, towards the hours of the morning, and roused with difficulty at the sound of a throat cleared outside her tent. She gathered herself hurriedly, and coming outside found her first lieutenant, Cheadle, awaiting her urgently with a fresh dispatch.

She broke the wafer and read the message. Mingled relief and regret: she felt at once that a hand had been stretched forth to save her, only a little too late. "Mr. Cheadle," she said, "pray send to Captain Winslow and the other captains. Admiral Roland requires us at Folkestone without delay. It seems Bonaparte means to try another crossing, and we must be there to stop him."

LIEUTENANT GARDINER'S London establishment was familiar, comfortable, and quiet; an ideal setting for a wounded soldier, and the careful and affectionate nursing of her aunt Gardiner shortly saw Elizabeth past the crisis of the feverish wound she had taken at the battle of Shoeburyness. But it left her with cause for regret at her surroundings: there was little remaining to distract her heart from its unfortunate occupation.

When Napoleon had been trampling the fields of Britain, and she and Wollstonecraft had nightly to scour the Channel for any sign of French ships trying to bring over more soldiers for his army of conquest, she might thrust Mr. Darcy from her mind with some success. Lying in a peaceful bedroom, with a view over the small garden tenanted by no-one more exciting than her youngest cousins, who furthermore had been abjured to keep quiet to avoid disturbing the convalescent, the matter proved considerably more difficult.

In vain did Elizabeth order herself to forget. The worst danger to her health past, consideration for Wollstonecraft's anxiety had won her the liberty of leaving her bed and going to the covert for a visit, once each day, but this having been accomplished, Captain Bennet was ordered back to her bed with very little to do, and all of that sadly uninteresting and faded. She had always been used to find diversion in many places, but now books slipped out of her hands and slid to the coverlet with their pages unturned; trays were carried away with only a few mouthfuls taken; and she answered with so much distraction and restlessness, when her aunt sat with her, that Mrs. Gardiner began to be afraid for her health, and speak to Lieutenant Gardiner of calling in a physician.

But Admiral Roland came to her first, a fortnight after the battle, with a better medicine. "Bennet, you have a listless air," she said, with her blunt kindness. "The hole those Frenchmen put through your side has healed nicely, so I dare say you had better get back to your duties: it will only be light work for a while now, for all of us. In any case," she added, "you will need to be on your feet Thursday week. They are going to make you Knight of the Bath: it will be in tomorrow's Gazette."

Elizabeth had at first to overcome the most extreme astonishment at this news before she was able to express the sentiments of gratitude and delight natural to any young officer in like circumstances. We may well suppose these increased by her complete lack of anticipation of the honor to be bestowed upon her.

"No, you may thank General Wellesley," Admiral Roland said, when Elizabeth attempted to thank her. "The Admiralty would be delighted to go on pretending we don't exist, except when we are in the air, but he has no notion of brooking it, and you may well imagine the lot of them are ready to give him anything and everything, at present."

Such an interesting piece of news could not fail to lift Captain Bennet's spirits—and Admiral Roland's prescription was eagerly seized upon; as soon as her visitor had gone, Elizabeth rose from her sick-bed and dressed in haste, meaning to go and share the news with Wollstonecraft. But she had no sooner finished tying her neckcloth when one of the servants came to her room, wide-eyed, to inform her that a lady had called upon her, and demanded to see her at once.

"A lady?" Elizabeth said, in some puzzlement.

It was indeed a lady: the card upon the salver read *Lady Catherine de Bourgh*, whose name was only dimly familiar—some struggle was required before Elizabeth recalled that Mr. Darcy had an aunt, of that name. "But whatever can have brought her to see me?" Elizabeth said, wondering also at the lack of propriety in Lady Catherine's coming to call upon a stranger in so insistent a manner, without any introduction to establish the acquaintance. But she could not refuse a relation of Mr. Darcy's, and though wishing nothing more than to be gone, she shifted her clothing once more to put on a morning dress, and descended to greet Lady Catherine.

She found that noblewoman, dressed with far more grandeur than was appropriate to the occasion and the hour, standing stiffly by the mantelpiece in the sitting-room and inspecting with a disapproving expression the handful of small watercolors displayed upon the walls therein, which were not fashionable but merely the handiwork of Mrs. Gardiner's children. "Ma'am," Elizabeth said, and only just remembered to curtsey, instead of bow.

"You are Miss Elizabeth Bennet?" Lady Catherine demanded. Elizabeth admitted it. "I am Lady Catherine de Bourgh—I am, indeed, the aunt of Mr. Fitzwilliam Darcy, and his nearest living relation. Having said so much, I fancy I can have left you in no doubt of the cause which has compelled me to approach you."

"Your ladyship is quite mistaken," Elizabeth said, with increasing reserve; she could not wish but to like any of Mr. Darcy's relations, but it was impossible to excuse the brusqueness of Lady Catherine's manner. "I cannot in the least account for the honor of your visit." But no sooner had Elizabeth spoken than she forcibly recalled the terrible extent of French depredations in the final weeks of the war, and alarm made her forget decorum—she took a step into the room and cried out, "Mr. Darcy is not—your nephew is well?"

But Lady Catherine only colored with anger. "Let it be understood at once, Miss Bennet, that I will brook neither impertinence nor insincerity," she said. "You will not claim the right to make such an inquiry of me, while denying me my rights to demand an accounting from you."

Reassured that she could not have received this answer, as peculiar as it was, if Mr. Darcy had been seriously injured, Elizabeth had now only to be baffled. "Your ladyship must excuse me from willfully provoking any such charge. I can only assure you once again of my very sincere confusion, and urge you to speak plainly."

"Very well, Miss Bennet," Lady Catherine said. "My character has always been of a forthright nature, and if you will insist upon evasions, I will meet them with frankness. My daughter and I were forced by the invasion to leave our home in Rosings Park, and seek a refuge with my nephew at his home in Derbyshire. We found him very altered. He would not at first confess the cause, but when I had questioned the servants, I learned that Pemberley had lately been compelled to house a host of dragons and aviators, and that *you yourself*, Miss Bennet, had formed one of their number, and were, indeed, serving as an aviator yourself. —Well? Do you deny this shocking report?"

"I do not," Elizabeth said, her temper rising at the tones in which Lady Catherine uttered the name of *aviator*.

"And you avow it so brazenly! That you have sunk so entirely beneath reproach!"

"If I could consider myself to have done so, in serving my King, I might indeed feel shame," Elizabeth said. "But I cannot, and if your ladyship means to speak insultingly of the Corps, I must beg to be excused from any further conversation."

"Not so fast, if you please!" Lady Catherine said. "You shall not escape me so easily. I have not come to reproach you for staining your own character and reputation, which must be the business of your own family, but that of a gentleman of irreproachable honor and ancient family—I am speaking of my own nephew."

Halted by this accusation, too close to those she had leveled against herself, Elizabeth did not immediately quit the room, and Lady Catherine seized upon the opening thus afforded her to press home her attack. "My inquiries further uncovered the most appalling intelligence, surely a scandalous falsehood, that through the association thus unavoidably thrust upon him, you had practiced upon him—you had enticed him—to such lengths that he was on the point of making you—*you*—an offer of marriage.

"I could not insult my nephew so far as to broach the subject with him. I knew it must not be the truth—I knew he would never commit so great an offense against the propriety and reputation of his family. But I have been resolved to confront you, as soon as the unsettled state of the countryside should allow it, and to make plain to you that your wiles shall never achieve this disgraceful alliance. Now what have you to say for yourself?"

"Nothing whatsoever, to one so wholly unconnected to me, and who has not scrupled to offer me every form of insult," Elizabeth said, and only the very strongest feeling for Mr. Darcy prevented her from giving a harsher answer. "Your ladyship must excuse me; I can endure no more." She left the room without waiting for another word, shutting the door firmly behind her, and ran directly upstairs to her room, where she paced the narrow confines of her chamber in great disorder of spirit, as conscious of guilt as Lady Catherine might have wished, if from a very contrary motive.

That Lady Catherine thought only of her nephew's reputation in the eyes of the world, and cared nothing either for his virtue or his happiness, was manifest, and her ill-bred insults invited no answer but scorn. But Elizabeth could not ignore that *she*, too, had safeguarded only the first, and wounded the latter. Mr. Darcy had been willing to set aside the opinions even of those nearest to him, whose opprobium he must have known to expect. He had not counted insurmountable all the practical difficulties which the match would entail, nor should he have. How many women endured with courage long separations from their husbands, gone to sea or covert, and counted the joy of irregular reunions a sufficient recompense?

She had not matched that courage. She had chosen certain misery and vice for both, from the hollow motive of preserving his uncertain chances of future happiness, and her freedom from obligation. But what were those chances? That Mr. Darcy might be expected to marry a woman of superior wealth and rank than herself, was hardly to be doubted. But he had never yet shown himself inclined to do so. That his wife might be expected to devote herself to his interests was equally certain, but he had not made an offer to a woman who could do so. Observers might be amazed that with all his advantages, Mr. Darcy had made a choice so little calculated to improve his comforts in life. But surely she had no right to choose decorum over honesty, and make her duty an excuse to avoid the censure of the world.

In sudden decision, she put off her gown, and dressed again in her flying-gear. A chair bore her to the gates of the covert, where Wollstonecraft eagerly called a greeting as soon as she had come into view. "You are dressed for flying," the dragon said joyfully. "Are you better today at last, dear Elizabeth?"

"I am, my dearest," Elizabeth said. "I am quite well, and I mean to prevail upon you to take me up—indeed, I hope you will not mind taking me so far as Derbyshire."

"To Derbyshire!" Wollstonecraft said, her slit pupils widening orange a moment. "Oh! I should be delighted. Perhaps you have heard from Mr. Darcy?"

"I have not," Elizabeth said, in repressive tones, but Wollstonecraft only gave a knowing nod of her head.

"You are quite right, of course we must call upon him," the dragon said. "It would never do to neglect the acquaintance. Perhaps he has not yet heard of our victory."

"Scheming creature," Elizabeth said, affectionately, and went to speak with Captain Winslow and to acquaint him with her design of going into the North for a few days; having left the formation in his excellent hands, and having spoken with her first lieutenant and her ground-crew master, and visited her wounded men, she felt herself at liberty to set forth, and went aboard, well bundled against the chill, which if it were not as appropriate in Wollstonecraft's opinion as having set forth in a diaphanous muslin gown and an excessively long and draughty cloak, at least was surer of safeguarding her health.

The flight was not sufficiently long as to tire Elizabeth, after her long weeks of rest, but quite enough to make her anxious for the reception she might find. That Mr. Darcy's heart was likely to be fickle, she did not in the least fear; but it did not seem to her unlikely that he might have thought better of his intentions. "If he should reproach me with having shown an unpardonable indifference to his honor and my own, how might I defend my conduct?" she privately asked herself, as Wollstonecraft stretched her wings, and found no satisfactory answer. But she felt strongly that she owed him the chance to renew his addresses, even at the risk of learning he no longer wished to do so.

Wollstonecraft came down upon the far shore of the lake, with its beautiful prospect upon Pemberley, at Elizabeth's request; she desired at once the chance of composing herself better during the walk towards the house, and to give ample warning of her arrival. But the second aim made the first impossible; when she was only halfway around the circuit of the lake, a break in the trees permitted her to see the master of the house leaving by a side door, and coming quickly along the very path she walked, before he was once again hidden from view. The remainder of the walk did nothing to soothe her spirits. Every step drew her nearer to a final confrontation, and she was sure he was only beyond the next tree or shrub many times before he at last appeared, his hands clenched by his sides and the expression of his face grave and drawn.

He started when he saw her, and instantly cried, "You are very pale—you have been ill," with so much alarm that Elizabeth forgot her first embarrassment in assuring him she was well, and wholly recovered. "But you *were* wounded," he said, low, and she had to confess it; somehow her hands had come to be clasped in his, and he stood with his head bowed over them, and Elizabeth could be stifled no longer.

"Mr. Darcy," she said, "I hope you know I would never reproach you, if you had thought better of the sentiments which you expressed to me, this past December." His head lifted, as she spoke, and he fixed his gaze upon her so intently as to make her avert her own eyes, to maintain her countenance. "My duty remains unchanged, and with it every obstacle in the way of my having the power to offer any man a respectable or a comfortable home, nor have I possessed for years a character which might be compromised in the eyes of the world in such a way as to lay demands upon any man to to repair it. But nevertheless I cannot permit the answer which I gave you, on the occasion of our last meeting, to stand. I am ashamed of having made it. No further word will pass my lips upon this subject, but I would not have you think I do not esteem and value you more deeply than any other gentleman of my acquaintance."

"Captain Bennet!" he said. "—Elizabeth!" Although he was too much surprised to express himself very fluently, he did not long leave her in any doubt of his desires and by what means he felt she might best ensure his happiness. A small bench was to be found among the trees a little further along the path, overlooking the lake, and to this place they repaired and sat a long while together, discussing the arrangements for their future. They agreed upon it that Mr. Darcy would shortly take up residence in his house in London, where they would marry, and that they should together wait upon Mr. Bennet at Longbourne the following day, to acquaint her family with their intentions and seek their consent to the match.

"But I am afraid you must first apply to another authority: I certainly cannot marry without Wollstonecraft's permission," Elizabeth said, her spirits now restored enough to laugh, and they went arm in arm to the dragon waiting expectantly at the end of the path.

"Yes, Elizabeth may marry you, if she likes," Wollstonecraft said in judicious and somewhat lofty tones, but when Mr. Darcy had parted from them, to return to the house and share his happiness with his sister, before Elizabeth should join them for dinner, Wollstonecraft very nearly knocked Elizabeth down with a congratulatory nudge, and said gleefully, "And you *shall* be married by special license, of course. Oh! Elizabeth! I do not think there can be a happier dragon in all the world."

(art by Agnes Hartman)

Author's Note: A drabble is a story of 100 words—and while there are many debates on how strictly the limit should be observed, for purposes of this collection I have kept to the exact number.

*L*AURENCE FINISHED COUGHING THE LAST OF THE water from his lungs, rolled onto his back in the sand, and looked up. The tall, broad-shouldered woman who had hauled him out was gazing down at him with some amusement: there was a puckered scar down her face. Down the beach, Granby and Tharkay were helping the gasping tourist out of the water: he looked rather shaken, and deservedly, having ignored four separate riptide warnings all posted. "Very heroic," she said. "But next time, perhaps you had better work out a way to keep from drowning yourself, while you are about it."

(art by Al Lukehart)

STARS GLEAMED OVERHEAD WHEN THE EGG ROCKED ON its cradle. The attendant robots did not stir with excitement; they were not programmed to do so. But they came fully online immediately, monitoring the situation, ready to intervene if anything should go wrong. The enormous trees stood silent round them. The egg rocked, then cracked; another crack, and the dragonet's head broke the shell. He drew his first breath of alien air and blinked wondering upwards at the pitch expanse, the spray of stars beyond the leaves. The robots moved to offer him the feeding vat. He knew their voices already.

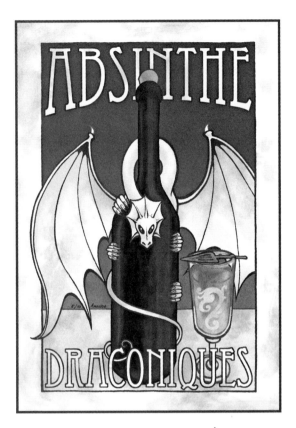

(art by Amanda Sharpe)

THE HUMAN CLUB, BELOW, WAS FULL OF RAUCOUS music and shrieks of laughter, but upon the roof small serving-dragons went back and forth to fill silver bowls set out at comfortably wide intervals. From the heights of Montmartre, the city was at once distant and all around, lit up brilliantly. "So much has changed, Madame, surely," one of the dragons said to her, inquisitively. He had a line of feathers running down his spine, a mingling with Incan blood.

The dome of Les Invalides shone golden in the distance. "I will have the absinthe," Lien said. The pain remained unaltered.

(art by Amy Thompson)

THE FRENCH AVIATORS WERE CALLING TO ONE another and to their coughing beasts, coaxing them to put on their armor; the process would require another hour or two. Laurence at once wished them gone, and yet they were the last hours of his liberty remaining. The last hours of his life.

Temeraire was silently and relentlessly furrowing the bare earth with his talons. Laurence said softly, "I might ask to borrow a Bible." Temeraire did not believe, he knew, but he had no other comfort that was his to offer.

"Of course, Laurence," Temeraire said, equally soft. "Read to me."

IN THE ARMY PAVILIONS ON THE YELLOW RIVER'S BANK, THE red dragons were singing a song of war, loud and sonorous, of mountains and ten thousand miles unrolling beneath them. Her father's heavy leather coat weighed upon her shoulders, and the wide belt with its straps round her arms and thighs rubbed with every stride. Her hands were sweaty around the long shaft of her war sword. Surely they would see through her at once.

The official with his scrolls heaped around him never looked up. "Your name?"

"My father is Hua Hu," Mulan said.

"Report to the third pavilion."

(art by Caitlin Johnson)

"I DO NOT SEE," TEMERAIRE SAID IN SOME IRRITATION, after the poem had been read, "why this Hrothgar fellow had to build his house directly atop the dragon's cave, and while naturally no one could approve this Grendel fellow's eating thirty people, I cannot call it astonishing that when you push into someone's territory and set up a tremendous noise every night just as he likes to go to sleep, that he should make strong objections. And I dare say he did not eat thirty people, or anything like, either; if he were so big, how did Beowulf slay him?"

(art by Erica Lange)

*L*AURENCE HAD GONE ALOFT AT THE AGE OF TWELVE, and had spent nearly all his life aboard the airships of Britain, the groan and hiss of the engine and the faint digestive rumbling of the sacs a familiar music; before he had ever gone aboard Temeraire's back, he had clambered over their bulging surfaces to repair rigging and had even stood up with his boots half-sunk to see the land and sea spread out beneath him like a map. But he had never conceived even so of a city built vertical, full of dragons flying, and ports established in mid-air.

(art by Erika B. Xochimitl)

"WOULDN'T IT BE LOVELY TO GO ROUND ALL the world?" Elsie said, looking at the poster eagerly.

Hollin's attention was caught more by the prize: one thousand pounds. He was getting on, and he had been puzzling himself a great deal lately how to keep poor Elsie from some miserable breeding ground when he could not go aloft anymore. *The triumph of the machine!* the challenge screamed, but when he squinted at the rules written small, they said naught was required but visiting the ten cities on the route. "I suppose you can fit on a boat," he said thoughtfully.

(art by Jason Lauborough)

JANE PULLED HER NECKCLOTH LOOSE AND WIPED THE blood from her face as best she could, then tied it up round her head. The dead Frenchman was hanging over the side limp in his straps. She bent down to unclip him. His body tumbled away into the billowing gunpowder clouds below.

She stood up and found Caudec staring. Her cheek throbbed viciously, and she could feel the flesh trying to gape, but she could still see out of the left eye: a stroke of luck. "The boarders?"

"All repelled, Captain," he said. For the first time, the title seemed unforced.

(art by Jennifer Rahier)

THE MOON WAVERED ON THE SURFACE OF THE water, distantly. The cistern was very low. Kilit shook his head, golden rings jingling, and went aloft in a wide circling loop that took him over all the great sprawl of the city, moonlight on the canals. The air smelled of rain, but it had smelled of rain last week, too, and the rain had come, but not enough. Not enough had come last year either. The granaries were growing low. There would not be enough food for the dry season, not for everyone. He would have to hold the rites again.

(art by John O'Brien Schroeder)

THE TOWERS OF THE JIAYU GATE WERE LARGE enough that Temeraire could stand upon them, and the two red dragon guards had respectfully slipped away and left him alone. The scrubby ground about the gate did not recommend itself, it was only pebbles and dirt. There was no appealing scenery: nothing to remind him of the fragrant gardens, or the soft green mountains. Temeraire bent his head. Down below the customs inspectors were making a great noise over everything which his crew wished to bring out of China. He wondered if any of the goods were sorry to go, too.

(art by Karena Kliefoth)

"NO, THESE ARE FOR *MY* SUPPER," DEMANE SAID sternly. The rabbits were not big enough to make Kulingile even a mouthful, but he still thought anything Demane caught was meant directly for his belly.

"Oh, very well," Kulingile said, and settled down while Demane set them roasting on a spit. The other aviators were all at dinner together, and Roland would say he ought to be there, too. Well, he was not going. He did not need them to say he was an aviator. He had a dragon for that.

When he slept, on Kulingile's arm, he dreamed of flying.

THARKAY SOFTLY FINISHED THE STORY OF THE BOY swallowing the dragon-pearl and going into the river, his mother weeping on the bank. Temeraire's eyes had closed. The waves lapped gently rhythmic at the ship's side. Laurence stood with a hand on the railing of the dragon deck, facing into the wide distance, his hair wind-blown. A stern quality had come into his face, this last year: in the fading light he was a statue gilded by sunset. It was a pang not unmixed with pleasure to look on him, as ever. Tharkay was glad the despair, at least, had gone.

(art by Kelly Nugent)

JANE HAD NOT MEANT TO LIKE THE FELLOW; HE HAD been described to her as very blue, and he was formal as any man she had ever met, in all conscience. She had asked him to dinner only to be polite, to Emily's captain, and to give him her countenance: there were any number of officers still bitter to have a heavy-weight dropped in a Navy man's lap, and her approval would silence some whispers. But she surprised herself to find, after two hours, that her pleasure in the conversation had not once flagged. And not in his shoulders, either.

(art by Kelsey Zilowar)

"ONCE UPON A TIME THERE WAS A SPLENDID KAZILIK dragon, who had heaps of gold and three pavilions, each larger than the last, and any number of dragons courting her, bringing presents from morning until night, all to gain her friendship and persuade her to form an egg with them—"

Temeraire flattened back his ruff. "That is not a good story at all, and there is nothing wrong with your wings, either; you can catch your own sheep."

"It is an *excellent* story, in my opinion," Iskierka said, "and I am busy; this is not easy work, you know."

Anatomy of a Celestial

(art by Kyle Bice)

*E*DWARD HOWE PUT DOWN HIS PEN AND STUDIED HIS work with a satisfaction so great he felt it nearly unseemly, and yet beyond his power to repress. The delicate spines of the wings, the outlines of ruff and tendrils, all accurately represented, and every bone which he could place with conviction based upon the external examinations which Temeraire had so generously permitted. Alas, he could not include any diagram of the mechanism of the divine wind: peering down Temeraire's throat had offered no illumination, and he would not stoop to speculation. No matter. The Royal Society would be delighted regardless.

(art by Kyle Broad)

"SURELY, LAURENCE, YOU CAN MOVE A LITTLE quicker," Temeraire said. "It will be days before I am close enough to claw at Lien at this rate."

"I am afraid it is rather difficult," Laurence said, sounding peculiarly underwater.

"Well, I will be patient," Temeraire said disconsolately. "At least Napoleon is smaller than you are," he added for consolation, peering across the murky and befogged field where Lien perched very awkwardly upon the Emperor's back. He had the insistent sensation, looking at the strange figure they made, that there was something quite wrong, but he could not quite work it out.

(art by Maarta Laiho)

*L*AURENCE HAD ALWAYS RESOLUTELY REFUSED TO express a preference for any particular familiar; when other mages of the Corps had spoken aloud of their hopes for great cats or gyrfalcons, he had kept his peace, and when pressed had only said he should be content with any beast that chose him. He did not intend to be discontented, or ever make his companion feel the lesser, if only the far more usual rat or crow made its appearance after the summoning ritual.

However, he felt now justified in a *little* dismay. Where was he to keep a fully grown dragon?

(art by Maria Nagy)

(An excerpt from a letter written by Matteo Ricci, February 1583)

THEY POSSESS AN EXTRAORDINARY NUMBER OF dragons, who are housed at night within the very precincts of every town and city, in large temples which are turned to the business of the state during the day, and where high-ranking officials receive petitions and give judgements while the beasts are out. A few either from age or ill-health remain sleeping in the corners, but no person shows any fear or concern about their presence, and so well-trained and docile are these creatures that they never offer harm to any person. Indeed some dragons are venerated almost as highly as their rulers…

JOIN, or DIE

(art by Michelle Brenner)

BENJAMIN FRANKLIN'S FAMOUS CARTOON WAS PUB-lished in 1754 on the eve of the outbreak of the Seven Years' War in North America to urge closer bonds among the British colonies, represented by the divided segments of the body, and their closest Indian allies, represented by the two sections marked with wings and draconic head, indicating the Iroquois connected to New York, and the Wampanoag and Narragansett and other Algonquian-speaking tribes to New England. It and Franklin's accompanying editorial were among the earliest arguments for the forging of a unified identity among colonies and tribes formerly disposed to consider themselves rivals...

(art by Nickol Martin)

KULINGILE PRIVATELY COULD NOT UNDERSTAND what so distressed Maximus, and some of the other heavy-weights, about him. He remembered himself as small and ungainly and sure to die; that was what everyone had said. "They will not be unkind to you," Demane said fiercely, when Kulingile ventured to say something, after they had been in camp in Portugal a week. "If they are, you will tell me, and we will soon set them straight."

"No one is *unkind*," Kulingile said, warmed through again. He did not care if anyone did not like him. No one had before, either: except Demane.

(art by Sam Pipes)

TEMERAIRE WAS A GOOD OLD EGG, MAXIMUS thought affectionately, as he padded back to his covert with his belly full, ears pricked and careful as he put down each foot. There were no squeaks of dismay from underfoot: he *did* like getting up and having his breakfast before the crowds were awake and scurrying about. Berkley was still snoring loudly in his cottage, a pleasant comfortable noise, and the ground-crew had not begun stirring. Maximus yawned himself and lay down in the large red-painted circle where the crew knew not to go, so he would not squash them by accident.

(art by Sarah Arcand)

THE JUBILEE PROCESSION WOUND AWAY FROM THE cathedral and through the streets back towards the palace: the marching troops, the great open carriage in front drawn by eight horses, and behind it the queen's dragon Gloriana with her head craned proudly upon her neck, leading five dragons trailing away in size behind her. Temeraire could not help but be pleased with the splendid display: a riot of color and glory; and better still, the road they followed was wide enough for dragons. But the ceremony over, he took wing to be alone, and think of what Laurence would have said.

THE NOISE WAS A PECULIAR ONE, AND LAURENCE did not know what to make of it; he had never heard Temeraire make it before—a sort of humming resonance, accompanied with a regular stamping that made the earth shiver. "Temeraire?" he called, doubtfully, and pushed aside the underbrush and came into the clearing.

"Well? Why is it taking so long?" Iskierka was saying, impatiently, as he parted the tall grass. One appalled glance was enough to make Laurence aware he had grossly intruded; he let the tall blades mercifully cover the scene and turned and fled hastily back into the trees.

(art by Tabitha Emde)

E OONOILON SANG DEEP AND RESONANT, HIS VOICE rumbling through the water, and Ilia sang back, swimming round his head in spirals, catching the currents that his great body made, cold and refreshing. Tomorrow the migration would begin, and there would not be time for play: they had a long journey to the winter waters ahead, with Eoo leading the pack. He knew the way. Ilia's mother often said she might sleep the whole four weeks and none the worse. But it would still be dangerous and long, and this year Ilia was a guard. She would play while she could.

(art by Tanya Thienpothong)

"WHAT? WHY NOT?" DEMANE SAID INDIGnantly, pulling his head back. Why not, as though everything were easy, and they neither of them had to be thinking of anything but themselves.

"And what do you suppose we are to do when Mother retires?" Emily said. "Don't be stupid. It doesn't mean we can't—"

But he was already getting up, his back gone stiff. "I am not going to *dishonor* you!" he announced, and Emily pulled her knees up and rested her forehead against them. It was not that she didn't like the captain, but he had *much* to answer for.

Artist Copyright Information